Museum of Stones

ALSO BY LYNN LURIE

Corner of the Dead 2008

Quick Kills 2014

Museum of Stones

LYNN LURIE

etruscan press

Etruscan Press
Wilkes University
84 West South Street
Wilkes-Barre, PA 18766
(570) 408-4546

 Wilkes
University

www.etruscanpress.org

Published 2019 by Etruscan Press
Printed in the United States of America
Cover design by Lisa Reynolds
Cover image © The Estate of Ralph Eugene Meatyard,
    courtesy Fraenkel Gallery, San Francisco
Interior design and typesetting by Julianne Popovec
The text of this book is set in Adobe Caslon.

First Edition

17 18 19 20 5 4 3 2 1

Library of Congress Cataloguing-in-Publication Data

Names: Lurie, Lynn, 1958- author.
Title: Museum of stones / Lynn Lurie.
Description: First edition. | Wilkes-Barre, PA : Etruscan Press, [2019]
Identifiers: LCCN 2018008124 | ISBN 9780998750873
Classification: LCC PS3612.U774 M87 2019 | DDC 813/.6--dc23
LC record available at https://lccn.loc.gov/2018008124

Please turn to the back of this book for a list of the sustaining funders of Etruscan Press.

This book is printed on recycled, acid-free paper.

For Andrew

Thank you:

Terese Svoboda
Noy Holland
Phil Brady
Andrew Koven
Barnett Koven
Franny Koven

Museum of Stones

I ASK THE NURSE to count his toes and then to count again. She holds a crumpled form in front of me covered in fine film, more embryo-like than human. I count five toes, then, five more.

Off to the side in a stainless-steel basin is the bloody cord, a red veined mass, oblong.

Someone says his nail beds are turning blue. Two nurses rush in and wheel him away. The masked doctor sewing me together tells me not to move. Already I can't remember the color of his hair or the shape of his forehead, and when I close my eyes, I see his face suctioned beneath transparent wrap, like meat.

Mother-in-law knows I do not eat meat, yet brings me chicken broth and saltine crackers. In her house each egg is cracked separately and inspected to see if there is a fleck of blood in the yolk or plasma. If any abnormality is detected the egg must be thrown out.

Returning to my village I crossed by bus from Ecuador into Peru. Seated beside me was an Indian who spoke little Spanish. He wore no shoes and his homemade crates stuffed with chickens blocked the aisle, while others strapped to the roof with twined rope shifted with each bump, the sound echoing inside the bus. He was unable to sell the chickens in Ecuador, where he had hoped they would bring a higher price.

It was midnight when the bus reached the town underlined on my pencil-drawn map. A man from Florida answered the door. He showed me how to light the stove and offered me leftover chicken. I prefer eggs, I said. He sold me three for one hundred *soles*.

I had to walk across a central courtyard to get to the bathroom and when I woke up feeling ill I darted across the cold stones half-dressed, my hair knotted in a bun. I was sure someone was watching from a half-drawn blind. The rest of my stay I slept in my clothing and kept my shoes and toilet paper in front of the door.

The hostel had been connected to the neighboring church and once served as the nunnery. Now the wall between the two was cemented on both sides, making it impossible to move from one to the other. A brass plate screwed into the stone at the entryway says that for five decades the nuns cared for sick children at this very place.

Draped in yellow disposable paper my husband stoops over a rectangular Lucite box. A bonnet covers his hair and blue booties are snapped over his shoes. We take turns reaching inside.

He lets me go first. I am sure it is because he is afraid. What if after touching the tiny body with the tips of his fingers he was to find the skin had gone cold?

Neither of us mentions the chapel on the other side of the hall, although it is impossible to block the wooden cross from view. Initially I do not understand the volume of people coming and going throughout the day. Yet, after a week in that windowless room, where night and day are no different, I too am drawn to its upholstered pews. What holds me back is I would have to explain I was hoping, just maybe, I could believe.

With my fist clenched I wind my forearm sideways through a heavy sleeve of plastic. My hand, smelling of rubber and disinfectant is all he knows of me.

He does not yet have a name. My last name is sealed inside a plastic band fastened to his ankle. I would have preferred the wrist, but it is no wider than a straw.

Lights hum. Equipment starts and stops. Across his chest is a tiny tower of gauze. Our eyes travel box to box but do not focus on any one station. Neither of us has room for more sadness.

I am afraid that by the time the nurses and doctors arrive to our pink-rail-thin baby wearing a pale blue hat they will have no empathy left, certain there is only a finite amount.

The mother of box number three taped pictures of family members to the far side of her baby's cubicle. Even if he or she could open its eyes it could not see that far.

The photograph facing me is of a cat curled on a window ledge. Sun streams through the Venetian blinds, stenciling a striped pattern over the orange-matted fur. Nearly hidden in shadow and off to the corner, a young boy wearing a bright red shirt is reaching.

As soon as they were born, the women in the village drowned the baby kittens in the irrigation canal. Otherwise they became a nuisance, carrying fleas and ticks, which spread diseases the children were especially susceptible to. Since the time of the Incas they raised large rodents as a source of protein, but no matter how hungry they might be, they had no interest in eating cat.

My husband perspires. Beads of condensation form above his upper lip and dot the length of his forehead, his face grey-hued. He helps me onto the three-legged stool we have been allotted. As I shift across its hard surface, my skin, at the place of the sutures, throbs. I imagine the edges pulling apart, a crooked path of blood etched into my underwear.

My eyes are fixed on the monitors. I know the range of acceptable numbers. The way the graph should read, the feared colors, the ominous flat line.

Mother said, not the mattress, the side bumpers, or the linen. Father clarified, only the frame. This half-offered thing, reminiscent of so many other half-offered things, and I slump into the glider's tufted seat, upholstered in a repeating pattern of dancing dogs.

I would like to be on that cushion now. Instead I selected something far less expensive: three black and white zebras twisting on translucent twine, having read the experts who claim babies are far more responsive to black and white.

A cherub-faced resident points to a picture in his textbook. There are too many sections and competing diagrams and not enough spaces between the words. My eyes resist moving left to right, habituated not to drift from my son's screens.

It is your job to explain, I say, my voice breaking the nearly pin-drop silence that is the norm in this room. The incubator staff and parents look over at me. I stare back and most turn away.

We are so many it is possible the doctors and nurses will, with one quick waive of a hand, dismiss us.

Guests stand too close and hover too long. Once the naming is over, the water sprinkled and the silly outfit removed, I take my son to the backyard and sit on a faded plastic swing.

My husband carved his initials into the seat when he and his sisters played here, the factories' smokestacks skirting the horizon then, just as they do now.

A strong wind draws black billowing exhaust from the paper mill towards the ocean. Sulfur and other particulates, dense and acrid, hover overhead.

For his seventh birthday he selects a wooden swing set with a blue tarp for an archway, strung taut between two poles. Not long after, he takes it apart piece by piece, jamming the thick metal screws into the dirt, arranging the beams and the rounded climbing bars like matchsticks along the swing set's former footprint, each fractured post a decomposing monument to a childhood he wanted no part of.

Miss Wells sat me next to Billy Grabard because I knew the alphabet. Poor Billy, she mumbled, he can't tell one letter from the next.

I helped Billy draw a straight line on the dotted penmanship paper, watching his knuckles turn white as he held tightly to the pencil. He struggled most when it came to making the two half-moons in the letter B.

A week passed and Billy still hadn't been to school, then two more. Eventually the janitor cleaned out his desk, putting his books on the shelves and his pencils in the storage cabinet.

I asked Miss Wells what happened. She said Billy climbed to the top of his swing set and couldn't get down. Why, I wanted to know, didn't anyone help? All she did was shrug.

Mother said Billy's neck got caught in the joint where the top arm fit into the bottom pole. When he tried to pry himself free, there was too much blood. He was slow, not good at thinking things through. He should have been supervised. I wanted more, but she was walking away.

When everyone was at music I asked Miss Wells one more time. She took my hand and led me to the back of the classroom. I told myself to pay attention, but all she said was, please, take a pecan cookie.

At every backyard swing set I saw Billy pinned at the neck, his white Keds with the blue label dangling. Even though his feet stopped moving, specks of red continued to dribble onto his white shoes.

I could not participate in the game the other children played, hanging a stick-like figure, body part by body part, on a hook drawn like the letter **S**, and when the bell rang for recess, I did not rush outside to grab a swing.

From my bedroom window I watched two men in a pickup truck carry Billy's swing set away. The longest pole was his torso and the two on either end that supported the structure were his arms and legs.

The art teacher showed the class how to fold a piece of white construction paper and where to make the first cut. We concentrated as we guided our rounded scissors with the rubber handles along pencil-drawn lines. Even still, a boy would cut his hand. The bloodied cutout wasn't displayed. Yet even the simplest diamond shape or sloping line was taped to the art room window. After ruining three sheets of white paper Billy succeeded in cutting a snowflake suitable for hanging.

Counting three across and two down, I found my snowflake as the bus pulled into the parking lot. Billy's didn't look like snow and now that we knew he wasn't coming back I wanted to ask Miss Wells to take his down.

Streetlights illuminated the falling snow. My future husband and I made our way across college walk lightly dusted in shimmering mica. I thought, confetti, the way it is tossed from rooftops in victory parades.

A bouquet of deep-colored roses, red wine, a bath in an antique tub, two matching terrycloth robes draped over a pedestal sink. Black and white subway tiles, finely veined, three missing.

In the honeymoon photographs I pose beside bronze busts, a woman's profile sculpted by Picasso arranged geometrically on a promenade overlooking the sea. At each rendering the structure and symmetry of her face is more distorted, and in the last she is a mawkish, half-human, half-bird, falling into the water.

When my great aunts saw me their voices formed a chorus, confirming that the features of my face were the same as their long dead mother's. But because there were no pictures of my great grandmother, I was never able to confirm if what they thought they saw was even close to the truth.

The eldest focused on the shape and color of my eyes, while the youngest, a sculptor, drew in the air the curve of my chin. She took my hand. You can feel it, she said, as she moved my palm over her cheekbones and then across mine. They are nearly the same.

When she leaned in, I breathed deeply, hoping to hold onto the odor of mentholated cigarettes, hair spray and sweet perfume. These are smells I still associate with power.

She owned a dress store of women's eveningwear and allowed me to run up and down the aisles, touching each gown with the palm of my hand, memorizing the feel of velvet, brocade and lace, but it was the word *organza* I loved. Sometimes she would begin a sentence that way. Organza, are you ready for lunch?

When she packed to leave on buying trips I hovered nearby, in case she might decide to take me along. In my closet I kept a small bag of clean underwear and socks, a notebook and my set of colored pencils.

I waited for her postcards of animals, ornate buildings and exotic flowers, but the stamps in colored ink from Italy were my favorite. She searched for starched crinoline and fine handmade lace, returning with swatches of fabric stuffed into pillowcases.

Near to the border with Bolivia in the department of Puno, I found a postcard in the Indian market dated 1931. Seated on the ground, a woman works a floor loom. The caption on the postcard is: *La Tejedora,* The Weaver.

I looked through the vendor's leather satchel filled with glass plates. There was one of a bride wearing a woven shawl loosely draped over her head.

Master weavers, he said, used a four-stake loom, saving their best work for this particular garment, a wedding veil that covered the top of the bride's hair. He called it a *lliklla*.

A woman selling corn nearby tried to describe the loom to me in Quechua. What I mostly understood was the drawing she made, using her crooked index finger to trace the outline into the road dust.

I taped *La Tejadora* to my bedroom wall made of dried mud and pressed straw. It followed me to subsequent bedrooms where I positioned it over chipped paint or holes where others' pictures had once hung.

Even though I knew I would not find my Aunt in the postcards I looked at the details hoping she might be there. She taught me how to remove the stamps using the steam from the spout of the teakettle. Once free, we slid each stamp between two pieces of wax paper, sealing it with the tip of the hot iron. I catalogued them in a bound book of handmade paper, arranged alphabetically by country.

My son keeps records of 'matters important' in a leather album. There are the letters he received when he was sick, and neatly folded sheets of paper crammed with lists of his numerical codes.

There was nothing sentimental about Mother's wedding dress. But, by selecting it, I reduced the amount of time I had to spend with her, searching the reduced racks, going from sale house to sale house, arguing over price, knowing whatever I selected it would be too expensive.

Buttoned and cinched within Mother's yellowed gown, its borders too voluminous for my small frame, I begged my childhood friend wrapped in tight-fitting black silk with shimmering sequins to switch.

As my father walked me down the aisle, I realized he had in a different decade unbuttoned the same dress. I tried to steady myself by digging my fingernails into my palm. The cut I made was long and deep. By the time I noticed it was too late to blot the red away.

Specially laundered, the dress came back in a long, white box vacuum-packed in durable plastic. Mother kept it in the attic alongside the disassembled metal bed frames, the mattresses and green plastic matching suitcases. Discarded objects arranged as if someone was living upstairs in that windowless space, putting them to use.

As we brought each thing down, Father cut his wrist on a piece of broken glass. Whitish-yellow, he clutched the railing of the pull cord ladder. Mother came into the bathroom where I was washing and dressing his wound. She dropped the box at my feet and said, you are to take the wedding dress when you leave.

I was preoccupied with my father's skin. It was like tissue paper. This thinning of the skin was the beginning of the ending of his life, yet Mother nattered on about the box at my feet.

I carry the box with the dress to the beach and unwrap the veil and train. Even the bra I wore is inside. I place it under the bodice after positioning it in the sand and wait for the tide to take it.

It does not float or drown but sloshes back and forth.

Covered with sand and seaweed and entangled with broken bits of seashells I do not want it, but I also do not want to leave it.

At the reception my mother took me aside. She said, your mother-in-law is dressed in all white. I had no idea this was a problem.

There on the other side of the threshold are the new rooms I will inhabit, the heavy furniture upholstered in muddy colors, dishes too precious to use, and the people I will now be expected to call family.

I buy a salmon-colored dress and bone slingback shoes, a leather skirt with pinking shear trim. A strand of fake pearls. Styles and colors I never wore before, and even though they are expensive, I do not take them off the hanger or remove the tags, but leave them pushed to the far end of the closet.

My sister and I played dress-up when we were supposed to be doing our homework. She was the expert at make-up. I could turn her curly hair straight and my straight hair curly. Make me unrecognizable, even uglier, if no one will know it is me. Don't worry, she said, one day we will be able to leave.

There were the dresses that had belonged to our grandmother in the attic, the silk ones with matching hats and mother's hoop skirts and saddle shoes, the bright pink tops.

My husband takes me to a favorite place from childhood, and as he is explaining he doesn't know why he calls it Peggy's Cove, a wave splashes over me. I lose my footing and slip waist deep into the freezing water. He helps me over the moss-laden rocks as the cold creeps upward, numbing my legs. He doesn't hear when I ask if we can leave, my voice faint against the breaking of the waves.

I sprawl across the back car seat's stained fabric, rife with the odor of my father-in-law's cigar smoke, a habit my husband later takes up. At night I see him on the deck, the red burning tip of his cigar, as the half-arc of light travels from his hand to his mouth. He drives in silence thinking I might sleep.

Feverish, I drift in and out of sickly sleep, unable to recognize anyone or any of the places that come to me. My husband brings me medicine and the prints of the pictures he took at Peggy's Cove. We are flipping through when his mother calls him. I place the stack on the nightstand, turning the top one over. It is of a large seagull with its mouth wide open. Between its teeth, a silver fish squirms. The sky is blocked by a swath of low flying birds.

His mother wants to know if he will join her for a round of golf. Eighteen holes will take all day.

Laundry piles up. I shrink clothes and bleed colors. Other houses have toy bins, cupboards filled with food. Rarely can we find the tennis rackets, the balls or winter coats. Everything is stacked or shoved into whatever space we can clear.

No one I know repeatedly runs out of toilet paper or uses crushed lasagna noodles to make a kind of spaghetti.

My husband and I fall into a deep sleep mid-morning and wake to the smell of burning plastic and rubber. The nipples and bottles I am sterilizing have melted and merged, forming a sticky mess at the bottom of the pot. A dark smoke stain in the shape of peacocks' quills forms on the white tiles above the stove.

I open the windows wide and by the time I collect our sweaters a pigeon has flown inside. Leave it, my husband calls from the hallway where he holds the blanket in front of our son's face, protecting him from the smell of burning plastic. It will be drawn to the light and be gone by the time we return.

As we walk aimlessly I worry more pigeons will fly inside, that one will asphyxiate, and if it were to die in the nursery it would be an omen.

By the end of the day we are too tired to stay out any longer. Strapped to one of our chests in the corduroy carrier, our son has not rested but has flailed his arms and banged his tiny head back and forth.

I use the broom to shoo the pigeon toward the window. It flits about and when it flies out, I slam the wooden frame. Pieces of chipped paint fall across the sill. Beneath the white is another layer, pale blue like the cracked shells of the robins' eggs my sister and I would find under our favorite climbing tree.

One year we watched a baby break its way out. For three weeks the mother came and went bringing food. By the fourth week all of them were gone.

Pigeon shit in his crib, dribbled over his stuffed animals and the hand-knit blankets, greenish yellow with flecks of red leaching into a white oozing paste. His full diapers nearly that same color.

The nightly news reports that formula cans sealed with lead may have leached lead into the liquid. It is the only thing he has ingested his first three months. Could it be why he is the first to get sick and the last to get well?

The first year I know everything he drinks and eats, what he sees and hears, where he feels pain. Then I lose track.

A man, tall and blonde, blue knapsack slung over his shoulder, walked down my path. The rattan walls of the latrine did not keep the wind out. I mounted colored advertisements torn from TIME magazine on planks of wood and hung them over the gaps. When they became weathered by the wind and rain he replaced them with glossy pictures of cars and fancy kitchens, stories from the news. Nancy Reagan on a boat heading toward Ellis Island, a soybean harvest in the Great Plains.

The cover of the children's school notebooks showed Peru as including part of Ecuador as well as the northern tip of Chile. I ripped the cover off and added it to the latrine wallpaper.

We took a bus to the coast, swallowing our malaria pills with cheap red wine he poured into his leather wine sack. Embroidered in jagged yellow stitching and red twined cord, *Espana* was written across it in script.

On the other side of the mangroves, having plied our way through in a rented rowboat, we found a small island with black sand. Not thinking about how close we were to the equator we stayed all day. That night the only relief was to float in the cold saltwater. I was in a light sleep when I startled myself awake, the roots of the mangroves, like the gnarled hands of an old woman, had risen from the water and had wound their way around my neck, making it difficult for me to catch my breath.

Our machetes and rubber boots lined the interior wall of our two-room barn. Every evening before bed we hung our ponchos from a hook. He was in the habit of straightening them when he walked by, making sure the bottoms did not brush against the loose dirt floor.

I dreamed of a tribunal of men, their parchment pages spread across a worn table. All but one had feathered pens. They questioned the assembled held against their will, their hands and ankles bound. A small-eyed man with translucent skin tossed burning oil from his lamp into the face of a crying child, then ordered them to walk until they found a place where they might be allowed to stay.

We washed our clothing in the irrigation ditch on a stone worn flat by all the others who had been beating their woolen ponchos, their patched trousers and hand-loomed skirts at this very place, ever since the canals first filled with water, three thousand years ago.

News came out of his battery-powered radio, rarely in English. The U.S. invaded Granada. The Argentine army deployed to the Malvinas.

He led me to the ice field in time to see a single star falling before melting snow in a tin cup. Then left me and went the rest of the way alone.

Condors nested in the rook above our campsite and when the largest birds flew away at dusk, the current from their opened wings – a span so wide I wished for more light so I could see – dislodged pieces of the rock face. The debris landed in the cavern below, producing a hollow echo.

I strained to hear the sounds of the tiniest birds that had been left behind.

Inside his two-person tent I fell into a deep sleep and woke to the muffled cries of what sounded like a child in pain. I crawled outside and looked into the woods surrounding our campsite but was unable to trace where the cries were coming from. Then the snow began to fall in lines, making it difficult to see even the nearest trees.

When the storm passed I saw our tiny barn below, a lone building in a place of barley and wheat, where the landscape, even in the rainy season, was never more than a washed-out-beige, the llamas and alpacas that same color, too.

Evangelical music from a nearby village played, broadcast by Oklahoman missionaries who had toilet paper and a flush toilet. They built a mega-church that towered above the mud huts with thatched roofs, none of which had electricity or running water.

When sunlight streamed through the stained-glass windows it cast an eerie green-blue shadow on the whitewashed walls. Disciples mounted a radio transmitter and antennae to a pole that soared higher than the steeple.

The blonde man bought me a green typewriter at the market and a kitten with fine black hairs around both eyes. It shook so violently we tried to warm it in our homemade oven. Still, it died that same night.

We were in the habit of sleeping entwined in our woolen hats and hand-knit socks we bought in the market, the heavy flannel from home. But the draft whistled through the cinderblocks and we would wake most nights shivering from the cold.

It was his idea to plant the apple trees behind the school, which, when I returned years later with my son were producing red and yellow fruit.

The Narnia Chronicles were the only books he brought with him. I was never able to get beyond the first chapter. He tried reading to me each night but after the first week I asked him to stop.

Years later when my husband read the sports pages out loud, this too, I did not appreciate.

We took a helicopter over an ancient glacial field and as the ice deepened the layers became dark blue, almost purple. Over time the steep banks receded and now appear on the map as nothing more than a needle's drop of water.

He was on a trek when I packed until I could fit nothing more into my duffel bag. I hitchhiked a ride with a trucker transporting wheat to the capital. Had I stayed any longer it would have been far more difficult. Already, I had postponed leaving for too long.

As soon as he entered the house and saw that the books had been picked over, he would know. In the next room I imagined him closing the empty drawers I had left hanging, half-opened.

Likely he looked for a note, but would soon have realized I did not leave one. Later in the evening he might have taken a walk along the abandoned railroad tracks. The memory of the smell of eucalyptus burning for the evening fires almost made me want to turn back.

He sent a letter telling me he sold my blue bicycle. Someone else must be riding it now; her feet stuck out horizontal to the pavement as I learned to do, after being bit by one of the mangy dogs that rushed into the street. For two months I underwent rabies vaccinations and feared the dosage wasn't correct or the serum had expired, losing its potency. I saw my body floating above me and when I looked down what remained was an outline of a human form sheathed in white.

Gathered in a banquet hall I remember the trip to Peggy's Cove and the sensation of my body leaving me. Prematurely the bride's dressing room door opens and a whirl of white floats into the room, filling the aisle. It is not Peggy, but her sister wearing Peggy's wedding gown. A man coaxes her inside.

Eventually Peggy enters as the bride. In a Jewish wedding the groom is required to walk seven times around the seated bride to be sure she is the woman he has chosen. The night ends without any of us seeing Peggy's sister again.

Other toddlers put my son's toys in their mouths. When they leave I boil everything they have touched in a large soup pot. He is too young to have a favorite so there is no risk of melting any particular one.

The day we move into the dark pseudo-Tudor in the suburbs we find fresh piles of shit in our bedroom. Raccoon feces emit noxious fumes, sometimes so concentrated with the rabies' virus no bite is needed.

The shudder of the appliances, the wind howling through the eaves, a falling branch. I am sure the raccoons will return, open our windows, turn doorknobs, pull down our sheets and get into our bed and his crib.

The previous owners dumped camphor in the crawl space to disguise the smell of feces and urine, replacing one toxin with another. I hire a man to sand the attic floor and another to varnish it. During the winter, so the fresh air can circulate, I keep the attic windows open. When my husband complains about the draft I do not tell him I am responsible. He would have insisted I close the windows.

My son stops sleeping. Each night he stands in his crib and cries. Eventually if he is able to drift into his partially slumped, partially standing sleep, his screaming wakes him and the cycle begins again. The doctors do not know what it is or how to manage it.

Raccoons or flying squirrels, I am convinced, must have returned to breed in the crawl space above his room. I hire exterminators, trappers and animal experts but no one finds any evidence.

The nurse's job is to let us sleep. I can't escape the sound of her pacing, her slippers shuffling along the pine floor. Even when I leave my room and go downstairs, I hear her. I should tell her that continuous walking does not lull him, that I have spent nights on my feet, but then I realize his crying has stopped.

Does she exhale without thinking where her breath will fall, or does she channel the marijuana smoke towards his face? When she leaves at the end of the week, the price of our sleep too costly, his crying starts again.

A doctor prescribes medicine I administer with a dropper but will not authorize a refill. I can't convince myself it is acceptable to smoke marijuana or burn it in my son's room as if it is incense.

If I put him in his car seat and drive at a steady thirty miles per hour, he sleeps, but if there is traffic he wakes up screaming. The trick is to keep going. I take the same route each time, convinced he has memorized the intervals of straight road, the stop signs, the duration of each light.

In his insomnia his eyes sink further into his head. His skin turns grey. The sound of lullabies, the turning of the black and white zebras, none of it has any effect. I play Brahms. The Rolling Stones. Mahalia Jackson.

Mother had us pack an overnight bag. The launch took us to father's new sailboat moored at the far end of the harbor. A strong current pressed against the starboard side, pushing us farther from shore. Crammed in my bunk I hoped for sleep, but as the waves picked up I was sure the boat had become untethered.

I rocked back and forth humming. Maybe I dreamed. I was lost and running through a swamp blanketed by rot. Tree branches reflected on the water's murky surface appeared as swords drawn from their sheaths. A dense canopy of moss crisscrossed the sky.

Underneath my bed I stashed books and shoes so no one could shimmy beneath and lay in wait, whereas, under my sister's bed, she piled the secrets of her teenage life: rolling papers and weed, risqué clothing including the high-heeled shoes and makeup stolen from expensive department stores where mother shopped but never took us.

I would wake with the sensation I was not alone, that someone had settled into the dark corner or the other side of the half-opened closet door.

Not remembering the chair that was always in the same place, its rattan seat frayed, I saw it as a man and the shirt draped over the frame as his tangled hair. Too paralyzed to turn on the light, I gripped the sheet and waited.

Lightning struck the house across the street. The family huddled near the fire truck wrapped in blankets. Rain was turning the smoke an eerie orange.

White and red lights flashed through the window at a dizzying speed and danced across the wall. I didn't know how my sister slept through it.

What had they lost in the fire, the two turtles their daughters named, Barbie dolls, and glittering hair ties? Now that their things were wet or burned I asked Mother where would they sleep. My parents didn't invite them in or bring them dry blankets.

Blue velvet lined the inside of the box and an oval mirror was glued to the top lid. The mirror reflected the image of a ballerina in her white crinoline and pink ballet shoes. She turned to the repeating melody of *Somewhere Over the Rainbow*. Her arms, face and legs were sculpted in white porcelain. I played the song so many times my mother threatened to take the box away.

My son prefers tiny boxes that stack, an antique dresser with many drawers, a ribbon cabinet and great-grandmother's button container. He spends hours rearranging the contents, and if I interrupt he bangs his head on the table. When the head banging is over he starts again, but only after returning to the very first step in his memorized sequence.

I ask the first of many neurologists what is wrong with a baby that does not sleep. Doctors, he says, are trained to see horses, not zebras. Does he mean the former are ordinary and the latter are anomalies? I am so sure my son is a zebra I beg him to look again.

The doctor traces his index finger along my son's cheek. What is it? I jump up. What do you see?

A child in his waiting room cannot sit still. Every limb is in motion. With the precision of a perfectly calibrated machine, the boy moves colored building blocks around the room. When there are no more blocks in the bin he gathers what he has distributed and begins again. None of the other children approach him. It is as if they know. His mother is the nervous one, chewing her fingernails, her eyes fixed on the illuminated EXIT sign. She stands and reaches for her jacket and pocketbook, checking her surroundings as she carefully folds her newspaper. Looking left then right before quietly walking in the direction of the door. Something causes her to reassess, and she slinks back to her seat.

The nurse whispers to the nurse-in-training, it is a fatal insomnia. When she tries to reason with the boy he becomes so enraged three adults are required to pin him down.

I close my son's bedroom door. I imagine leaving him alone in the house, imprisoned by the four sides of his crib, each locked in position, his diaper overflowing, the wet running down his leg. I do not intend to return.

Other times I am fastening him into his car seat as I prepare to drive over the side of the bridge at the center point where the distance to the water is the greatest.

Did great-grandmother trekking the Carpathian Mountains with her sick son strapped across her back, in search of a doctor, finding no one who would help, her desperation heightened by her son's trust, consider plunging headfirst into the valley?

Grandfather's sister took care of him when his mother worked in the family store. She pushed a chair against the window and piled pillows on top. He spent hours in that seat, watching the children in the courtyard, and even in his old age he remembered the birds and the way the light illuminated the dull wood table hewn from a single stump.

A mother drowns her children in the bathtub. Another goes to the river, while a woman in a southern state makes news for smothering her littlest child first, before moving on to her next two, and when there are three listless lumps beneath foam pillows she goes into the kitchen and prepares a cup of tea.

Hoping to leave the house without having to provide an itinerary or be obligated to bring my son along, I move with concentration. If I can get to the door that leads into the garage without the creaking sound of the wooden floor alerting him, I know that from there I will have no trouble turning the doorknob soundlessly.

As the breeze picks up, plastic bags and debris caught on the jagged rocks that line the shore wave like tattered flags. Discarded cigarette boxes litter the sand.

Women missing front teeth call to children that race after seagulls, kicking up sand and yelling to each other. One boy aims a rock from his homemade slingshot while another pretends to be the newly shot bird, dropping to his knees.

I collect our son and his many things as a poorly dressed marching band assembles. Its metallic sound rises above the thrashing of the waves.

Tears pool in my eyes – the forced parade, the gray sky. His favorite picture book of beloved animals, bears, raccoons, pigs and ducks, but the made-up one, the Yeti, is his favorite, wild man of the snow.

Flurry and Bart and the all-white one, Ling-Ling, but the only one he cares about is Teddy. As insurance I buy an identical Teddy but he will not go near it naming it Not Teddy. He asks me to move Not Teddy to the top shelf.

A matching game no longer interests him and I offer the tin of flour. It is, I say, similar to sand. But it is sand he wants. Instead, I open a can of ground coffee.

I taught the villagers to make carrot bread in the *panaderia* donated by the Swiss government. Each morning they churned out rolls made of white flour and water that were given to the school children free of charge. At first it was difficult to get the carrot bread to rise because of the altitude. After numerous tries we were able to produce a perfect loaf, but it was impossible to convince the villagers to like the dark-colored, dense bread.

He mixes the flour and the coffee in the tin measuring cups and empties them, building cylindrical mounds across the kitchen floor. There is a pattern to his placement, one tower dead center in the middle of each ceramic tile, ten and counting.

When he starts screaming and rubbing his eye I rush him to the sink and pull back his eyelid. Floating across the blue is one granule of brown. I tilt his head sideways and dribble water into the corner of his eye. If I can set the speck afloat, I might be able to dab it away. As he tries to grab the glass from me I envision him with a pirate's patch, blind, in the left eye.

I am overcome with sobbing each time I get into the car. The kind that causes my whole body to shake, making it difficult to catch my breath.

Somewhere between the house and the sandbox the key to the back door fell from my pocket. I sift carefully through our newly completed town of sand. When I do not find the key I have no choice but to level the whole thing.

It is the time of day when the vultures circle the nearby dump, blocking the sun and turning long swatches of ground black. I convince myself someone has found the key and is waiting until dark to enter the house.

The basement has ten windows and two sliding glass doors, perfect entry points for intruders. Each evening I check even though there is no reason to believe anything has changed. The wind, I reason, could have blown out a window or the gardener could have rammed his lawnmower into the glass.

My son and I sit on the floor of the Museum of Natural History under the blue whale, discussing the way his muscles contracted to propel him through the water. In the semi-darkness we strain to hear the underwater sounds, sometimes muffled, other times perfectly clear. In every city we visit we go to a Museum of Natural History or Science, but by far this one – the one we know almost by memory – is the most remarkable.

He doesn't like to leave, not even to go to the planetarium, but after hours of looking up I convince him there are other things to see.

He slides to the end of the plush upholstered velvet seat and leans his head back. We wait for the lights to dim. From the southern hemisphere the Milky Way is a wide causeway of sparkling mica schist, bordered by diamond-studded mountains.

He whispers, outer space has many dry planets. HD 209458b and HD 189733b are two that are worth exploring.

The clouds, pale wisps of white, skeins of wool, slowly unravel. He gives them names. Accumulatory, bluefalling, collidicus.

He runs across a wooden bridge. When he is close to the arch in the climbing bars I yell, Duck. He yells back, Goose.

I help him collect molting caterpillars. He studies the sequence of black dots across their backs and sketches the patterns into his notebook.

At night he chases fireflies, trapping them in a glass jar with a metal lid my husband riddled with holes. He records the intervals between the flickering.

The carpool is coming.
I don't know how to swim.
I signed you up for archery.
Sign me down, he says. I've no interest in arrows either.

He selects a book on Morse code and memorizes it before we leave the library. I tell him it is possible to check it out and take it home. He shakes his head. I'm sure it's because he does not want to upset the order. When he is finished he returns the book to the shelf, making sure the numbers on the spine are in sequence with the other books.

Likely the mother of the boy tells him it is an opportunity to see the train from an angle no one else has ever seen. She knows the time of the train's arrival and calculates how long he will be able to sit in the cold, taking into account that the train might be a few minutes off schedule.

As the gravel presses into the back of her legs, she says, watch the metal of the wheels, feel the charge of electricity, see the flash of light.

Following the incident that particular train is removed from the schedule.

No realtor is able to sell the house where they lived. The windows are boarded and padlocks are placed on the front and back doors.

Each day we crossed the railroad tracks that ran parallel to the Pan American highway to get to and from our barn. A newborn lamb was tied to a stake too close to the tracks.

I lifted the lamb into my poncho and took it back to the village, hoping someone had a lactating ewe that might save its life.

A mile up the mountain where only potatoes grow, we heard that a woman had abandoned her newborn daughter. In the early morning, before going to the fields, the woman next to us, who had no children of her own, hiked up the mountain, returning later that day with the baby strapped to her back.

My husband lifts my grandfather into the car. The wind blows open the back of his hospital gown. He is so thin I see the malformed bones in his left leg, the scars from childhood where the doctors lanced an infection in a place that then was Poland and now is Ukraine. Two days later my grandfather will be dead. I wish I had not seen it, that he was wearing a diaper.

Jumping up and down on my mother and father's bed my niece says over and over: Papa Ruby died.

He draws our family in stick figures holding hands, placing my red mark on the right side of my face across my lip and under my eye, looking as it does, as if a man with a large hand slapped me repeatedly.

Following the first session my birthmark turns the color of an eggplant's skin, then fades, taking with it some of the red. I had hoped for something to peel, desperate for some sort of proof it was leaving me. The course of treatment is longer than gestation, longer than infancy. It lasts his entire childhood. The doctor reassures me there will be no scars.

My burned and swollen face upsets my son. I am unconvincing when I tell him the procedure is less painful than being seen each day with the mark.

Years later my son and I meet a woman who walks all night to reach our free clinic in the middle of the Peruvian desert, guiding her daughter who, while studying catechism, lost her ability to see. The father barred the girl from entering the house believing she was possessed. She has a birthmark on the right side of her face nearly identical to mine. Her long braids are tied back with colored ribbon and she wears a black bowler hat that is the same as her mother's.

Anticipating a simple response, a doll, a pink sweater, a pair of Nike sneakers, I ask what sort of gift she would like when she wakes from her skin graft. The little girl says, a house. Their previous one, a tent made of tarp strung across bamboo poles, burned to the ground one of the nights her mother left her and her four sisters to go to the sea where she descaled and deboned the fish the fishermen brought in at dawn.

Likely the mother left an ember burning, maybe even intentionally, to keep her girls warm. The child we treat, her burns covering her face and neck, is the only one that survived.

Had I bought them a simple adobe house it would have cost $6,000 according to a NGO I contacted who worked in the area. A Swiss man in charge of the project confirmed that the deed to the plot of land the mother showed me was proof of legal ownership.

I never followed through, convincing myself it was too much money, that she was not my responsibility, further rationalizing there would be no electricity or water to the site, no protection from theft.

We called them freaks. Even still, I dreamed of running away with the midgets, the hermaphrodites and the bendable man and woman.

I studied my reflection in the hall of mirrors, preferring it to what I saw in mother's mirrored bathroom, her perfume bottles arranged on a marble shelf, the atomizer puffs screwed in place, her tubes of lipstick stretching into infinity.

The woman who sold the blonde man our meat referred to me as the one who is stained. The village elder was nicknamed *Mono*. He was lithe as a monkey. His neighbor, *el lobo*, was fierce, whereas the woman, who lived across from us known to cast spells, whose name I never knew, was *la bruja*. A witch in our village, like a witch back home, was depicted as flying on a broom handle.

La bruja stole a truck belonging to the Ministry of Agriculture parked at the entrance to the village. A functionary, dispatched from the central office, had come to seize the villagers' seeds, alleging they were diseased. She heard the men arguing and grabbed all of the seeds stored in the schoolroom before backing the truck out onto the Pan American highway and heading south.

Flyers announced the arrival of a circus. No one in the village knew what this was, but still, the children wanted to go. We piled into the back of a truck bringing a crop of carrots to market. As we got closer I pointed out the painted yellow and blue plastic eaves rising from the side of the mountain. The children turned their heads in unison toward the colored sky and together we heard the music of the organ grinder.

Indian families congregated on the other side of a wire fence, unable to afford the entry fee. The rollercoaster jolted and stuttered. The rubber pulls were worn and there were no seatbelts. I told the children to hold onto the railing no matter what and to not let go. It rotated and pitched sideways, but when it finally moved it was terribly slow, which I preferred. I feared the children might get stuck at the top when the thing unexpectedly came to a dead halt.

The elephant did not have the heft of an elephant. Its skin was crusted in sores and the flies from the nearby market buzzed around before burrowing into the oozing openings. While I tried for weeks to forget the circus, the children talked about it endlessly, the stories of what they had seen and done became grander with each retelling.

Years later I returned to the village and the children of those children wanted to show me something. I didn't understand what they were describing. We drove to the nearest town and they ran to a gleaming glass building with an escalator that climbed three stories. Their parents also loved riding it, and they, too, could have stayed for hours.

For Show and Tell my son brings his glass bear to class. The eyelashes are delicate wisps of opaque, luminous white, a shade lighter than the body. The glassblower offered him a chance to create a shape, showing him that breathing through a long metal tube was what determined the final form. He took him by the hand and led him to the fire. I was sure my son would breathe in, not out, that he would swallow the flame.

He is telling his class the heat in the room was tremendous, that the table and workbench were made of stone, when a classmate drops his bear. He stops speaking and gets onto his knees, scouring the floor, collecting each piece, crawling under every desk and chair, refusing help. When he is certain he hasn't missed anything he asks to go to the nurse's office where he spends the afternoon on her foldout cot, clutching to his chest his bag of broken bear parts.

The attic-ceiling fan shakes with such force I imagine it breaking free and moving through the hallway, catching up to him as he runs toward his room, shredding his flesh and the fabric of his fire truck pajamas.

To goad him into the bath I inflate plastic rafts no bigger than the palm of my hand. Red pill-like capsules dissolve into the water and the sponges inside expand, taking the form of animals. He balances the elephants on the pink floats and the hippopotami on the blue. A tsunami, he says, while clapping his hands under the water.

Two inflatables the length and width of a king-sized mattress are moored side-by-side in the middle of the camp's manmade lake. A boy falls between them and is pinned underneath, drowning before anyone realizes he is missing.

Camp is closed for two days and when it reopens the inflatables are gone.

A physical therapist tells me – our plates heaped with a pile of roasted pheasant shot that morning by our host – she works with brain-dead children, referring to them by some other name. One boy she massages every day lies in bed in the same house with the pool where he nearly drowned. She is unconvincing when she says he is responsive to her touch.

When I think she has finished I stand prematurely and even though I realize she is still talking, I begin walking with my dish and the untouched bird to the kitchen. I dump the bird into the trash and rinse the plate, leaving it in the sink. On my way back to my place at the table I stop and whisper to my husband, we need to leave.

The wake draws my son under with such force it pulls his bathing suit past his knees. While struggling to catch his breath he tries to run away, grabbing the elastic band that now hovers near his ankles. He takes a moment to turn around, and when he has our attention he scowls at us, his face twisted and angry.

My husband shows him how easy it is to motion for help while remaining afloat. I'm not afraid of drowning, he says, it is that water is unpredictable, I have no way to control where it goes or what it does, and, over time, it dissolves all things.

It is possible to date the photograph from the brief time during his childhood when he was not afraid of water. His body is distorted and the ripples illuminated by the underwater light make his abdomen appear as if it is slit open and his intestines are unraveling.

There were ten candles on my birthday cake, including one for good luck. I ate my slice the same way every year, avoiding the icing as I worked towards the filling. I scooped the chocolate buttercream out and placed it in the corner of the plate. When I had eaten all of the cake, I alternated between the icing and the filling making sure my last bite was icing.

I was ready to dip my fork into the pile of chocolate buttercream, scattered with roses in pink and yellow when my father reached for a forkful. I pushed his hand away but he pulled my plate toward him and started to eat. He ordered me to go to my room. I protested, after all, it was my birthday.

I was hoping mother would come to my defense yet her eyes would not meet mine. All night I worried I was not a good daughter, that next year Father would tell Mother I could not have a birthday cake.

Our neighbor rescues a baby raccoon and keeps it in a wire cage. She might have seen its mother get hit by a car, which is what she said, but it could also be she took it from its den. Once I searched her kitchen drawer for scissors and came across a page from a diary that was not in her handwriting, a laundry ticket that belonged to someone with a different last name. She, like my son, is a hoarder, a collector of things and a self-appointed guardian of animals. But this was worse. I was sure the raccoon she was harboring was rabid.

Raccoons in his picture books sit at desks, dress in red parkas, get on and off school buses. I tell him not to go to her house. We know raccoons. Our attic has the rank smell of animal urine and camphor. I fear the mother might return for her cub.

I am holding more of the phone than I should be, having ripped the base from the wall, the colored wires poking out of the fake maple paneling. I had hoped to destroy all future communications but as I pinch the wires into a ball, worrying about the dangers of the electrical current, I hear the upstairs extension ringing.

My son and I agree to do everything before dark as if we are living before electricity. I tell him about the barn I lived in tucked between two mountain ranges, high in the Andes, how we read by candlelight and rose with the sun.

Our pot of soup hangs from an andiron. We feed the fire kindling. Cross-legged, huddled on the rug with our legs and torsos tucked under a heavy blanket, we sip loudly, using wooden spoons with long handles.

We carried the propane tank we used to power our two-burner stove on our backs to town when it ran dry. The villagers couldn't afford propane and instead dug pits inside their one-room houses where they burned eucalyptus leaves. At the end of each day the women trudged home with the branches strapped to their backs. The walls of their houses were coated in thick black soot and most everyone suffered upper respiratory problems, especially the children.

My son and I use the last light of the evening to walk upstairs. I tuck him into his bed with the next day's clothing alongside him under the blankets, this way when he wakes, he will be able to dress before getting out of bed. We meet downstairs and feed the fire.

A colleague tells my husband that my husband is in the next round of layoffs. It now seems to have been gossip, but at the time we held onto each other, having no idea what to do next. In grief and in fear it is good to have a mate, less so for the times in between.

In the middle of the night I tell him we should leave before things get worse. Start over in a different place. Find another kind of work.

Eye level with the ledge of the wishing well, my son estimates that the quarters, nickels and dimes add up to a little more than twenty dollars. To be sure he hasn't missed any he walks the circumference one more time.

If I throw my Mickey Mouse bank at the window will it break?
It depends, I tell him. How much does it weigh?
The thing sails past my head. The window shatters.
I guess, he says, it weighs $3.79.

He will not go outside if there is a chance of rain.
He will not walk on wet pavement.
The sensation of water on his skin makes him wince. Bathing and brushing
his teeth become a struggle. He immediately removes a wet shoe or shirt
and keeps a stack of towels triple-wrapped in plastic in all four corners of
his room.

His father might have requested an uncomplicated boy. One who prefers
sporting events and plays hockey. Even one who sits endlessly in front of
video games.

Sometimes my son skips sleep working through the night, disassembling
and reassembling his inventions, a *helmular* phone--a receiver and
transmitter mounted inside his bike helmet allowing him to use the phone
hands free-- his precursor to Bluetooth. A security camera affixed to the
door that connects to the television screen and what he calls his abbreviated
keyboard. When he finishes he sleeps seventy-two hours in a row, not
waking even to use the bathroom.

I kneel beside him.
I take his pulse.
I watch his chest rise and fall.

He wakes up hungry. As I make a combination breakfast, lunch and dinner
I glance at him to confirm he hasn't changed in any discernable way.

When I can't sleep I drink cognac, then swallow prescription sleeping pills. I take so many I erode the lining of my mouth and esophagus. Eventually no doctor will write me a prescription.

Tenement steps. Chunks of concrete missing. Children's muffled screams. A filthy room. Two dishes, one glass, a bench made from a plank of plywood balancing on two cinderblocks. This man will sell me anything. He doesn't need a prescription.

It is irresponsible to hire a nanny who doesn't have much English. Over and over she says, "Fuckitfretfuckitfret," pronouncing my son's name Fret. She has frequent car accidents, nothing serious, backing into a wall or driving forward into a parked car. I have to get rid of her but I also have to be at work at 8 a.m.

She wears a seven-inch cross encrusted with rhinestones around her neck. Her teeth are stained, her eyes watery blue, her hair straw-colored. I can see she once was pretty, maybe when she was a young child in Costa Rica.

I know Guanacaste, I tell her. I passed through twenty years ago on my way to the salt beds. Lots of cattle, men carrying guns, tumbleweed and saloons, wire fences with animal skulls nailed to crossbars.

Her mother turned their front porch into a restaurant. They served local liquor made from sugar cane and homemade *bocas* of potatoes and onion, foods easily eaten without silverware. After working a twelve-hour shift in the slaughterhouse the men came hungry, often staying into the early morning hours.

There was a dark-haired woman with black eyes and tanned skin. She stood out because the baby on her back had blonde curls, a very white face and blue eyes. At the time I thought Peace Corp Volunteer, a backpacker on route to Guatemala. I stare at Fuckitfret's rhinestone necklace, the chain catching on her left breast. She could have been that baby.

My son begs me to stay or to please take him along. I shift my weight from foot to foot, trying to think of what to say. My head is splitting. When he knows he is going to cry and cannot hold back, he turns away. My vision blurs. Anyone, I reason, can care for him better than I.

It takes Fuckitfret all day to get our breakfast dishes into the dishwasher and only occasionally does she find time to make the beds. Laundry is rarely done and if she tries to process a load it sits wet in the washer for so long it needs to be rewashed.

My son scowls at me if I reprimand her. Years later he tells me she allowed him to steer the car, that they spent afternoons driving in search of a siren, following the sound, trying to predict where the emergency was. When they arrived they watched from the car, the windows rolled down, as an arrest was made or a fire put out.

Not until we are down to the last can of tomato sauce do I force myself to the grocery store. Walking the aisles I forget what I came for, going home with nothing more than a quart of milk and packets of ketchup.

Rather than wash the dirty clothes I shake and fold them before lining them edge-to-edge in the dresser drawers. If a grass stain or dirty sleeve is showing I revise the folding or reposition it in the drawer to keep the problem from view.

My son pleads with me to let him stay home from school. I drag him by his sleeve to the car. In the battle I slam the front door and it splits down the middle at the joint where the wood panels were pressed together at the factory. That evening before bed, because it is just the two of us, I take him to a hotel convinced it is a door begging to be broken into.

Facial tics so violent they keep him awake. One doctor finds their meter and rhythm fascinating. I interpret this to be a lack of empathy. The veins of my son's skin are so close to the surface I see the ghostly blue-green streams as they circumvent the red. With the skin stretched between my palms I hope the muscles will remember their original state of repose and return to it.

Metal clamps might hold his face still. To pin the skin in place, mounting it as if it is a butterfly's wings.

Involuntary movements in his arms and legs make it difficult for him to feed himself. A predominant symptom in a certain syndrome with a long and unpronounceable name, according to the latest doctor I consult. It has, he adds, been eradicated everywhere except Sub-Saharan Africa.

When I do not want to look at him I focus on the floor tiles, hoping the gouges in the linoleum will distract me. My husband is unable to sit across from him when his symptoms are the most acute.

He stays home from school. We play Monopoly. There are certain properties he must own, and when a game is over, he insists on another and then another. The game playing could go on all night. He does not become tired and he does not need sleep.

Hoping to break the cycle we decide to take him to Disney World. At Disney World he focuses on the way the bricks are spaced forming a moat around the castle. He sees patterns in the trees while all the other kids are hugging Mickey Mouse.

I tell him the school parade won't last more than an hour. That sometimes it is easier to go along rather than make a fuss. It's practice for when you are an adult, when you will be forced to do all sorts of things you don't want to do. Panic crosses his face. That can't be, he says, that's childhood.

The screen door slams on his face. I hate Halloween, the costumes, the make believe. As he empties his loot on the floor he asks if he can stay home and hand out candy instead. His face paint is smeared and his costume has shifted. The brown bear tail is no longer behind him but looks to be growing out of his side.

The day he is suspended from second grade he tells me the girl at the desk next to his emptied her knapsack and the insides – torn scraps of sticky gum wrappers, pretzel crumbs and stained hair ties – spilled onto his work area, but when the nearly full water bottle toppled, drenching his shirt and the front of his pants, he lunged at her. He hoped the teacher would kick him out of class, that he would be forever barred.

A child went missing from the one-roomed school in the center of the village. It was common for the teacher to not show up for work. Still, the women left their children and went to the fields, their hoes strapped to their backs, the sheep in front, moving faster when a branch of Eucalyptus, used as a crop, swatted them repeatedly from behind.

By nightfall there was still no sign of him. The next morning a woman crossing the Pan American highway to graze her goats found the boy in a ditch. His body was still warm.

I don't gather him in my arms. My hands are in my lap so he can see them and feel assured that I will not reach over to hug him, which might alter the feeling of his clothing against his skin, and although he has never said it, he must find me to be a source of germs.

We sit side-by-side on the edge of a stained couch as the latest doctor explains he is not crazy, because even though he fears water, he does not actually believe it has the power to dissolve him. But I remain unsettled and sense that my son, although susceptible to logic, is also unconvinced. How can the doctor determine what he or anyone really believes?

The doctor's head is suspended above his large mahogany desk, bobbing as he speaks. His tiny hands are so insignificant I wonder if they have sufficient strength to tie a shoelace. If they were my hands I would hide them or place them in my lap. Yet he keeps them on the desk, clasped and folded.

More than the doctors, my husband, or myself, it is the dog that saves him. She sleeps in his bed unless there is thunder, which so terrifies her she paces the length of his room. After a storm I find them asleep, nestled together, on the floor inside his closet, where the lightning is less visible and sound is muted.

On our early morning walk the dog wanders off and by the time I realize she is not behind me she is out of range. I run home and get my husband out of bed. Wearing boxer shorts, sneakers without socks and a thin windbreaker he scours the area around the frozen reservoir. If we cannot find her I am sure we will lose our son.

Each morning a teacher tutors him at our kitchen table. The rest of the day he rides his off-road bicycle around the yard with the dog strapped into the back basket. I come home from work and before I go inside I stand in the bike tracks he has etched into the snow and stare up at his bedroom window.

My husband brings him a white lab coat from work that hangs past his knees. I pin the sleeves to the elbows. My son inserts a plastic protector and three different colored felt-tipped markers in his shirt pocket and carries a small, lined notebook with a pen in his left back pocket.

From the top rung of a ladder, a handyman's belt doubled around his waist, he constructs a plywood frame then wraps it with chicken wire, stapling it in place. He says, after turning the sharp edges outward and hammering them into the wood, I'm ready for the parrots.

In front of the fully stocked cage he gracefully moves his arms as if he is signing to the birds. When he holds his arms steady they use them as a perch. This is when he is a master of stillness and even his face does not twitch.

An autistic boy in the neighborhood falls in love with his flock of parrots. When the weather is warmer we walk a pair to his house, having fitted a store-bought cage with a trapeze and hanging beads. The boy wants to take the birds out. My son places the smallest one on the boy's wrist, but when the boy howls, the bird flies away.

To console him I describe the color of the sky when the parrots migrated from the jungle across the Andes forming a sheet of green and red, that they would return six months later, nearly to the day.

The dog paces his room, scratches the wooden floor, pokes around his closet. When she hears the bus turning onto our street she runs to the front door and paws at it with such force I eventually have to replace the front panels.

My son's face is tear-streaked and there are tiny deposits of salt in his smile lines. He will not tell me why he has been crying. His long hair is tied in a ponytail with the red silk belt to my robe. My winter hat looks like a Bundt cake balancing on his head.

Over the phone the principal reads a prepared message.
Your son talks to himself and when he does no one can get through to him. It is as if he isn't there. Then names what he thinks the problem is.

I dial the hotel in a distant city where my husband is working. It's the middle of the night for him. He is schizophrenic, I shout, even though the connection is perfectly clear. When are you coming home?

There is so much snow that night the yellow and white awning covering our back porch collapses from the weight. It is the only thing I liked about the house. The metal sides that held it in place protrude every which way, like daggers.

When the cab pulls into the drive I do not let my husband inside. I pick up the first terracotta pot of swollen parsley stalks that have been thawing and freezing all winter and throw it against the brick patio, then bend down for the next one. I do not stop until I have broken every last one.

Dressed for a warmer climate my husband stands with his bare ankles covered in snow.

A man dismantles the awning and the rusted metal before plowing the patio under. After the remaining broken bricks have been hauled away it is as if nothing was ever there.

My son is as pale as the dog's blonde fur. He chose her over the others because she was the one that ran from us. All the rest piled at our feet, peeing on the slippery linoleum, whimpering.

The village elder brought me an all-black puppy with white paws. It took the puppy two days before adjusting to being separated from his mother. I named the dog for the mountain I saw from our barn.

Chimbo went everywhere with us until I left for good. When my son and I visited the village years later, *Chimbo* was tied to a pole, mangy and uncared for. When I said his name his tail began to wag furiously. I should not have left him.

My son wraps plastic sheeting over his bedroom windows to keep the moisture out, then nails wooden planks across the inside covering the glass completely. A labyrinth of chains and padlocks hangs from hooks he drilled into the plaster. Rarely am I allowed to enter, my husband not at all.

He does not leave his room, not even to go to his favorite store, the warehouse on the turnpike stocked with home repair tools. He knows what is in each aisle and what each item does. He met with the manager and suggested a more logical placement of the products providing a detailed diagram of what should be in each aisle.

The manager calls to tell him his plan has been put into practice and invites him to stop by. I do not tell the man I am unable to get my son to leave his room, not even to come to the hallway phone.

I find a trap door in his bedroom floor, a square carved into the wood that blends seamlessly. It is only when I walk across in a certain way that the creaking alerts me to the hidden compartment. Inside are the soapstone bears he picked out in Vancouver, the clay ones he sculpted in day camp painting them white and black, and the plastic bag containing the broken pieces of his glass bear.

Now that he is older what soothes him is the logic of numbers, the symmetry he looks for and finds in nature, finite shapes, and mathematical proofs.

1. All sides of a rhombus are congruent.
2. The intersection of the diagonals of a rhombus form 90-degree angles (they are perpendicular).
3. The diagonals of a rhombus bisect each other (they cut each other in half).
4. Adjacent sides are supplementary (they add up to 180 degrees).

In time we all fall on the wrong side of the equation.

One man tells the reporter he still smells burning flesh, how the smoke filled his nose and mouth as he ran down the steps, eventually reaching the street, having disobeyed the voice coming over the building's security system that, with authority, ordered everyone to stay in place.

The administration tells the students nothing. Parents arrive tear-streaked, clutching balled-up tissues. There is an unnecessary frenzy to find their children as each one is where he or she is supposed to be, bored and sleepy, seated behind Formica desks, knapsacks heaped at their feet.

The same pictures are broadcast all day and by evening the images begin to lose their impact. I replace them with my own repeating reels of disaster: my husband does not return. My son, too, is missing, stranded on the far side of a large body of water, littered with floating remnants of animal carcasses, a human skull.

Swimming in a hotel pool listening to an underwater radio my husband hears the news. It takes three hours for his call to get through.

After my son has fallen asleep a neighbor who works for the New York City Department of Public Health calls to tell me anthrax is the next form of terror. I do not know what this is. It would have been better if I hadn't asked her to explain.

Following the Lord's Prayer every Monday morning we were subjected to air raid drills and told to crouch under our desks with our knees pulled to our chests. My sister was especially terrified and every Monday tried to find a new excuse so she could get out of school.

A wall in the school's basement was repurposed in steel and iron. Students and teachers could live sealed inside for one month, safe from radiation. We never saw the rooms but imagined an Olympic-sized swimming pool, a basketball court and lines of bunk beds.

There were nights I slept curled under my desk. If mother found me in the morning crouched against the wall I told her I was searching for my Girl Scout pin.

Trying to get home by way of Canada my husband switches planes in three different cities and is prepared to drive, if necessary, from Montreal. He is able to get on the first plane to fly into the U.S. once the airspace is reopened. Our neighbor, the one who had coached the softball team, does not come home.

Tides of mud, three stories high were unleashed at the beginning of the rainy season, felling trees and sweeping cars and houses into a massive crater. The weather accomplished what the military could not, leveling the villages and the agricultural terraces that had been in place for centuries. With shovels and picks the dead were slowly uncovered.

My son is intrigued by what looks like a rear-view mirror at the end of a metal rod. The garage attendant checks under each car to confirm there are no explosives. He tells the man he is positive there is at least one blind spot.

I was accustomed to stopping at checkpoints along the Pan American Highway as I drove my rented jeep, the rear-view mirror stuck in place with duct tape. Military men, weapons poised, waved cars and convoys forward. Their presence was intended to reassure travelers that the roads were free of terrorists. Dressed in a bolt of fabric, a swath of navy wrapped around my waist and held in place with a woven belt, a hat with ribbons to protect me from the Andean sun, a necklace of coral plastic beads. My son, in time, will return to the same place.

The procedure room where the doctors and nurses prepare injections, make their incisions, and do their bloodletting has tropical fish and porous reefs painted in otherworldly brightness on all four walls.

Fluid clouding his brain is siphoned out, processed through a centrifuge, stripped of overactive antibodies and then re-circulated.

He is too old for fairy tales and pastels even at age seven, preferring stories of exhibitions to the Arctic and the Himalayans.

This pain, I whisper, will end. I watch the needle pull blood from him, the spinning of the centrifuge, the distillation of the plasma. I calculate the dosage, trace the route of administration, gauge in my mind his level of suffering and weigh this against doing nothing.

Eyes closed, he mumbles, bears hopping, bears swimming. I think the repetition is to distract him from the cold serum flushing his veins, but when I realize he is disoriented, I take his head between my hands and shake him, unconcerned with dislodging the needles and lines going in and out of him.

Eyes open but for a moment, he says, I am leaving.

He is the color of the sheet. His blood pressure drops. The nurse immediately stops the procedure. Trapped inside his illness, still unnamed, I am afraid that there may be no other doctor, no alternative procedure.

In that city of provisional tents, the only patient in the clinic when we arrive is an old man, naked behind a flap of canvas. Pinned to the cloth is a handwritten sign *Intensive Care*. A single nurse sits at his side and moves a fan of woven palms.

His legs are no wider than the tubing that runs from an oxygen tank to a mask loosely placed over his nose. His twisted body, the young nurse in turquoise – I cannot stop thinking about them. I ask the doctor if it is likely there is oxygen in the tank. She says, we don't let them die this way in the U.S.

Midweek I look but find no trace of the old man or his nurse. I should have asked the doctor, how do we let them die?

The orderly wheels my son's gurney toward the operating theatre. He is clutching Teddy. After the first injection they tell me to leave. The nurse hands me the bear. I refuse, insisting that when he wakes the bear must be with him under the covers exactly as it was when they took him away.

Hours into the operation, his skull open, I imagine the surgeons peeling away at something gray and coiled. I want to see the way the blood flows, the color of his brain. Let it be just one thing, and let that one thing be removed without damaging any other thing that allows him to be who he is meant to be. It is a prayer that I am repeating.

He begins to stir in the recovery room, his eyes not quite open. He asks me to please order a cheese pizza, and for the first time in years, I am hopeful.

I thought the use of alligator hide was illegal, yet I am sure his neurologist is wearing alligator loafers. The man's suits are equally as expensive. As I study his pant legs I am overcome with the desire to bury my right cheek in the fabric. I see myself dropping to my knees and running my face up and down his leg like a dog.

Ordinarily his flawless dress would have me looking for a different specialist, but here in this dark corner I admire his effort. Besides, there are only a handful of neurologists remaining that I haven't consulted. Their names are on a scrap of paper in my wallet behind my son's first grade photograph. There will come a time when this doctor runs out of ideas and loses interest. I have seen it before, and I will be forced to gather my son's medical records and schedule a consultation with the next name on my list.

Emergency lights flashing I double-park at Herald Square and run into a drugstore to buy black eyeliner. Using the rear-view mirror I blacken the skin beneath my eyes as I had done for him at Halloween when he dressed as a black bear.

I fall asleep in his hospital room in the chair beside his bed, forgetting to wash my face.

My mother drops by in her floor-length mink, powdered and perfumed, on her way to a holiday party. She asks me to get her fresh water, telling me my father is waiting in the car unable to find a parking space. There is a garage, I say, as I hand her the pitcher from my son's nightstand. She pushes my hand away. I don't drink tap water, and certainly not in a hospital. At the very least I need you to get me ice.

I take the pitcher and am about to go to the ice machine but turn back. The pitcher placed squarely on his nightstand, I stare at her wanting her to look back at me so I can scold her. But she will not allow her eyes to meet mine. When they finally do, she says, you need to wash your face.

The sign says Bank A elevators are for admitted patients only. I wait for an elevator from Bank B. Two orderlies and a stretcher are inside. On the stretcher is a mound wrapped in thick, green, opaque plastic, the color of a garden hose. The metal zipper running head to toe is secured and tied with thick wire. This is freight, he says, and motions for me to wait. Just hours ago, what now is freight was likely a passenger in Bank A.

Had they zipped the bag to contain the smell as the body moved to the morgue, or to keep the bacteria from migrating? And why the extra length of wire?

I drive to the hospital to relieve my husband. The dark pavement moves toward me and as I accelerate the yellow divider lines appear to rise from the roadbed, racing towards the windshield. The sound of my sobbing brings me back and I take my foot off the gas. What I want is to stop breathing.

Before the sales clerk's son jumps from the sixth floor of the mall's outdoor parking garage he stops in the dress shop where his mother works. Those who saw them recall nothing remarkable. A neighbor working EMS said the mother's statement was brief. "My son was ill. His life was impossible. There was nothing I could do."

A pounding on our wooden door before sunrise and the blonde man is asking the witch inside. She alternates between Quechua and Spanish, but what we understand is her daughter cannot move her head or open her eyes.

In her cave-like house carved into the rock face, the blond man tells her to get the neighbor, the one who owns a pickup truck. We need to get her to the hospital and we need to hurry. The witch comes trudging up the hill and tells us that the neighbor isn't going to town until the end of the week when he will buy *remolacha* seeds and that is when he will take us.

My best friend's mother took a lover when we were in tenth grade. He would be at their house when we got home from school. To get high quickly we smoked cigarettes and pot inside her closet with the door closed. Her mother made no effort to hide the empty wine bottles, to wash the goblets, or throw out the flowers he brought. The negligees she wore with him were tossed into the laundry bin with all the other household clothing, awaiting Thursday's maid.

A man called the house in the afternoons asking for my mother. She took the receiver into the pantry and closed the door. The light stayed on only when the door was left open.

When she came into the kitchen her cheeks were flushed and the first thing she said was, stop procrastinating and get to work. When I ignored her, she repeated it with greater emphasis.

On lonely long summer days my son and I sit on the park's green bench, the backs of our legs sticking to the paint. He orders vanilla ice cream no matter how many flavors and never adds toppings or varies the kind of cone.

The top scoop slides onto the ground with ice cream dripping onto his sandal or mine. We watch its slow glide. I feel tremendous sadness as it melts onto the piping hot sidewalk.

A street artist paints my son's profile on the side of the ice cream parlor. For years his image is on those bricks. When the wall is eventually whitewashed I am relieved.

Stones erode, chip and cleave, yet remain essentially the same.

I blame myself for my son not fitting in. I consider buying a ceramic rooster for the kitchen, a sweater with a holiday motif, and at the very least, I should volunteer on his birthday to bring festive cupcakes to his homeroom.

I beg a woman with cancer whose mind is blurred by morphine, whose house smells as if she already died, to test my son to see if she can explain why he is unable to complete actions consisting of sequential steps, or write his name, or tie a shoelace.

She intuits his love of the rhombus. Pentagrams, she says, have him work on pentagrams. The word is too sharp and he won't have anything to do with an uneven-sided thing. Really, I am concerned it is just one more way of accentuating his otherness. Before she dies, she tells me he is a genius. I am sure she has missed something. Even though I can see she needs to rest I keep asking her just to be sure.

My husband runs into his old girlfriend, Peggy. The one he was forbidden to marry because she was not Jewish, for which he was given a car in exchange. The car long gone, they are catching up.

Avi read the morning paper wearing white cotton gloves to not dirty his hands. Beneath the gloves each nail was manicured in clear lacquer. Before my oldest sister-in-law married him, my in-laws insisted he convert. William became Avi and his new last name retained only the first letter from the original.

The marriage didn't last and the family lost the only person able to wield a screwdriver, position a nail, or fix a cabinet. Before the divorce was final Avi changed both his names back to the original.

Who washed Avi's white gloves?

If I treyf up a fork by using a dairy implement to cut my steak, or a steak knife to cut through the butter, the treyfed up utensil must be inserted into the soil for a year before it is deemed kosher again. My mother-in-law has a garden of flatware for which I am largely responsible.

* * *

We follow the smell to the family room. The water in the aquarium is cloudy. There is no steady gurgling to the filter. When the filter stopped, did it take the fish all day to asphyxiate or did they go quickly? Mouths gaping, gills flayed, belly up, their skin and scales detached.

I hand my husband a plastic container. He scoops water and dead fish from the tank and pours it out the open window. My son says goodbye to each one alphabetically by name. Bananafish, Bestfish, Blueback.

When the tank is lighter we lift it from the stand and dump the remaining sludge into the garden. Some splatters onto the glass and puddles in the windowsill. We cover the remains of the fish with soil from the garden.

Every year following the last snowmelt, we find something: a glass ball that lined the ocean floor, a sprig of a plastic tree, the ceramic mariner in his salmon scuba suit that my son insisted we buy.

* * *

The woman that I imagine my husband is having an affair with gives him a desk lamp on her last day of work. Her husband has been transferred and he and their kids have settled into their new home. On their last meeting they play a final set of golf, a game I do not understand.

When my son is no longer interested in the swing he sits alongside me on the stone ledge. It is as if he knows. I weave myself a crown using the ivy that grows between the rocks, unaware it is poison.

The doctor administers something intravenously, prescribes steroids and creams. I sleep in the attic to avoid our king-size bed. My thoughts fluctuate between not scratching and the rules of golf.

I could benefit from a pair of Avi's white gloves, or a newborn's undershirt, where the sleeves fold over the nails. If the baby was able to direct his hand to the part of its body that needs to be scratched the shirt would keep him from doing any harm. I want to tear off my skin and then my husband's.

There are years he spends most Sundays on the golf course. When an oncologist says there is a higher incidence of cancer in golfers, likely correlated to the quantity of pesticides used on the greens, I ask my husband to reconsider.

As an oncologist I assume the doctor has a direct link to the dying, yet he hasn't considered the question of how people cope when death is near.

My sister goes to a car park motel with men she meets on the Internet. When the car enters the garage the door automatically closes. An anonymous person counts the cash and a machine dispenses the room key. An interior door leads to a room with a bed and a toilet.
I push my chair away from her and as she adds more details I inch further back. I see a stained bedspread, a rug worn thin, dried specks of vomit. Married couples, she says, also use the car park hotel.

Her first husband's mother broke into her house and stole her jewelry and mink coat. Why she had a mink coat in Mexico is a valid question. My sister had her arrested in Cuba where the woman spent five years in jail. None of the stolen items were recovered.

A flying chair shattered her nose when her husband, an alcoholic who mostly when drunk, threw dishes and furniture.

We learned he fathered a son with another woman while they were married. No one knew until the boy, who ended up in the same school as my sister's daughter, introduced himself as her half-brother.

Once he had a green card, her third husband, whom she never divorced moved to Spokane without her and found a job in a sardine factory.

My sister believes she inherited promiscuity from our great aunt, the one who wore false eyelashes and a thick layer of eyeliner, who had a closet full of brocade dresses, some sewn with silver and gold threads, others fringed with glass beads and feathers.

I stare at the marriage counselor's swollen ankles, an old age circulation and kidney problem. We share collective horror at his cascading flesh, which screams it doesn't matter what we do, life moves quickly and ends abruptly, all of it out of our control. But for now, it is the present tense that is killing us.

There are clay sculptures and nearly smooth metal coins in the counselor's glass case, adjacent to a desk he never approaches and a sage-colored blotter bordered by black leather with gold etching identical to one my father once had in his office. My sister lifted the border and tucked away from view was a photograph of a woman that was not Mother.

To ground myself, I focus on the first row of his facsimiles of ancient objects. Each aged to appear battered by the elements. I think we are to believe they originated in Mesopotamia.

I notice for the first time a beaker with a medicine dropper immersed into a yellow liquid on the far corner of his window ledge. It is not clear if it has been hidden or inadvertently covered by a plastic dust curtain. It is too thick to be urine. I wonder if it is plasma or bile, two substances I learned to identify when my son was in the hospital.

To stay present I lean into the couch and move my eyes left to right. The smell I previously attributed to the couch as we sank into its cushions, shot to hell, their damp mustiness filling the air, could it have been that foul liquid?

I do not like being questioned or watched, afraid my husband will learn or see something he previously failed to notice. He will store the information in his memory and call upon it when he decides it is time to leave.

My son's therapist explains there is nothing more he can do. Not wanting to lose him I tell him he has been a great help addressing my son's fear of water. He hands me a list of names of other professionals in the field.

I consider where I will inject the dealer's drug, running my fingers over the plastic pouch in my pocket. When it moves through my blood I forget my son, even though he is waiting for me at home. When I finally do appear, he will ask where have I been.

A cab driver stops at the crosswalk. His fingernails are seven inches long and look as if they are growing as the light changes. Certain it is Charles Manson I run into the alleyway and hide behind a dumpster. When I calculate enough time has passed, and I am sure the light has gone from red to green and back again, I return to the busy street.

Men mostly, deposited like falling debris, lined the irrigation ditches, having drunk so much *chincha* made from fermented corn that they appeared to be dead. Neither the cold nor the drenching rain could rouse them.

The women didn't look for a missing husband, son or father but stepped over them on their way to the fields.

All work ceased for one week in February and it was acceptable that everyone, including the women, drink *chincha* until they stumbled blind into a ditch.

The anti-drug poster that hangs in the guidance counselor's office features a needle. My son insists it be covered before he goes inside. Blood and plasma, needles and tourniquets, tubing and intravenous lines no longer frighten me.

I select a doctor from the yellow pages in a town I do not know. Scratches cover my face and back and the doctor wants to know who did the scratching. I tell him I have come for rehabilitation, not wound care.

My parents insisted I sit for a portrait. And when they move from the house where I grew up they tell me I must take the painting. I lug it to the car and store it in my basement.

I stab scissors into the middle of the canvas and maneuver them towards the eyes, which I cut out first, then the ears and lips that never resembled mine before deciding to turn it into a collage.

There is no red mark on the side of my face. Had the artist casually deleted it, or had he asked my mother if she wanted the portrait to be realistic, and she, without hesitating, said no, that this was not her objective.

I line the parts of my face in a row along the perimeter of the living room rug.

Black ice blankets the winding street. I careen across the yellow line and do not stop until the car crashes into a tree. I refuse a trip to the hospital.

Weeks later I crash my husband's car. It flips over and I free myself by crawling out the passenger-side window. I just miss hitting a doghouse. The dog peers at me. It is far too cold for him to be outside.

The grocery list is on the front seat of my car. To see if I have impaired memory I test myself. Eggs, butter. I can't remember anything else. What if I had killed their family dog?

I stay in bed seven days with the door closed. It is my husband's responsibility to get our son to school and field the daily phone calls from the principal. Each week the man threatens he will have no choice but to expel him. When my husband comes home from work and wants to discuss the latest problem I tell him I need to rest.

I backed out of the driveway while his classmate, a slow-moving boy, had one foot in the car and one on the pavement, but I never had a car accident with my son.

I crash the nanny's car. The side mirror hangs like a baby's loose tooth. One gust of wind. I hear it shatter on the pavement as I am being strapped to a board. Stay with me, someone keeps saying. I remember him, or was it her, asking questions, which, at the time I thought were to keep me from losing consciousness, but when the paper quotes me as acknowledging I turned left on a red light and was not wearing a seat belt, I realize why he asked. He could have made my answers up. There was no one to corroborate.

Noise is amplified. All smells nauseate. I do not know how long I have been in the emergency room. My husband arrives and arranges my discharge. An orderly wheels me to the revolving door. The sun outside is killing me.

The room spins and I am seeing flashes of neon. The doctor says, maybe an epileptic episode brought on by the concussion. I try to keep my head steady, moving just my eyes as I drift between banks of white.

My husband gives me one week to demonstrate I have a plan. Otherwise he and my son will move out. I sit down in front of the computer to compile a list. There are no keys; my son has taken the keyboard apart.

I find the letters stacked in the desk drawer. It will be a five-part plan. Following the 1, I write: find a Dr. 2. I want to write no more drugs but this requires two Os that I do not have. I collect the letters and drop them from above. They scatter like jacks.

The insurance company cancels my driving privileges for a year. It is likely this prohibition is what keeps me alive.
In the dim light of our all-beige living room where my husband and I rarely sit, I stare into the fire. It is snowing outside. He has taken our son to visit his parents. My lips burn and when I lick them they taste of salt.

Happy meal toys. Tape recorders, VCRs and CD players, stashed and stuffed in his closet, bookshelves, desk and wardrobe. A childhood of hoarding.

I save Teddy and Not Teddy and wrap them in layers of white tissue paper and put each in its own Ziploc bag. With the air suctioned out I see where I cut a tuft of fur from Teddy's paw. I remember sewing the swatch into my son's pajamas, the ones he wore in the hospital.

I save the guillotine he selected when we visited Mont Saint Michel. It isn't the child-sized replica but the one with moving parts that can be calibrated.

I fill the dumpster three times and when his clutter is gone, I feel better, but worry the purge might destabilize him, that he will not forgive me.

A week later he returns with my husband and doesn't comment on his newly cleaned room. Finally, I think I have done one thing right.

The neighbors' daughter enters our house at dawn and moves from room to room. She must have climbed to the top of our beech tree when no one was paying attention. Around dinnertime my son hears her calling.

A firefighter carries her down the way he would rescue a cat. As soon as her feet touch the grass, she runs the other way.

When the girl comes home from the psychiatric ward my son tells me her left hand has a tremor and her head is shaved. In summer he notices she has scars that look like cigarette burns running the length of her forearms.

My son's anaerobic digester is the jewel of his inventions. From the floor of the high school greenhouse the many-tiered contraption of tanks and tubing, gauges and wires reaches the ceiling.

On Sunday mornings it needs to be fed. I help him chop composted food scraps, which we load into his reverse-rigged garbage disposal. Maybe the disposal overheats or the wires become crossed but it bursts into flames. He runs for the fire extinguisher.

I begin rinsing mounds of paper towels in the sink when he warns me the particles should not become airborne, suggesting a vacuum instead.

When the smell of the composting garbage permeates the school's first floor the science department insists he remove it. The whole thing has to be taken apart, relocated to our garage, reassembled and kept running until he gathers sufficient data on methane output to document its success or failure.

He mounts the main tank on the wall and for reasons of gravity and gas production, feeds it from above. I have one job, to hold the ladder as he dumps the sludge down an elaborate tubing system that runs from the roof of the house to the garage through a half-opened window. When the slop lands on my scalp I let go of the ladder and run into the bushes gagging, leaving him hanging from the gutter.

My best friend and I cut and sanded soapstone at my parent's kitchen table, sculpting an imprint of a tree, an ashtray, Rodin's gate.

We lined the Formica table with newspaper, remembering to secure the corners with masking tape. I even placed the fruit bowl far from the metal sanding tools. The sawdust settled in the creases of the paper.

Father came into the kitchen through the garage, as he did each evening, and focused on the mess. He told my friend to leave. I watched her run across our backyard, her sweatshirt trailing behind. After I cleaned up Father sent me to my room.

My husband never built even a model airplane from a kit. He takes a piece of plywood and places it on the toy chest to create a tabletop after sanding the edges. He and my son assemble the interconnecting train tracks with hairpin curves, bridges and underpasses.

Mother isn't going to let my father forget he nearly killed her Friday night on their way home from the country club. She was wearing her diamond necklace and South Sea pearl bracelet. Maybe he was mesmerized by the blinking lights and didn't see the barricade, or maybe he was angry, gesticulating wildly as he is known to do. Or was it her constant complaining that so rattled him he just let go.

Injured, she carefully removed her jewels, placing each in the zippered compartment of her purse. Not until my brother arrived at the emergency room did she let go of the bag.

Her jewels are accounted for in a spiral notebook she keeps in her nightstand along with the list of which daughter gets what. Some entries have been erased so many times the paper has become transparent.
Father walks upstairs with his heavy step. Mother will accuse him of disturbing her. He yells at me to keep the line free because he is expecting an important call. Nevertheless, Mother has me phone the hospital to reconfirm that the emergency room doctor did not make a mistake when he concluded she was well enough to go home. She doesn't care that Father will force me to hang up.

Father is girded and poised to explain to the insurance company he was not responsible for the crash, having worked on his defense while the nurse ran mother's EKG.

When looking for evidence of neglect one needs to examine the feet of the elderly, placing particular emphasis on their toenails.

I said goodbye to my father by phone. A nurse in another state held the receiver to his ear. I did not hear even his raspy breathing. Out of kindness the nurse told me he understood, reassuring me that the last sense to go as one is dying is the ability to hear.

The train from D.C. to N.Y.C. stops in Metropark, New Jersey. My father is now buried here. It hasn't been a week when my train pulls into the station. It is near midnight and raining. The conductor announces the stop. I make myself open my eyes, wiping the drool from my chin. It is too dark to see anything but rivulets of rain running down the glass.

I had to look inside the casket to sign the funeral parlor's form, confirming it was my father. Mother and Father selected the coffin in advance, his clothing too, a white shirt, a patternless tie and blue jacket.

In the hospital they poured a river of red into him.
In the funeral parlor he was pumped with chemicals.

The train pulls away. I fall back to sleep.

Using the plastic fork and knife the cashier put into my bag, I eat directly from the take-out container. My husband's television is too loud. The grilled fish has a gray hue and the pile of boiled broccoli has lost its color.

Sirens, then horns of the diverted drivers, draw us to the window. A white sheet covers a section of the highway. Traffic is stopped in both directions and men using flares and wearing white gloves reroute the cars. One car is askew but hasn't sustained any significant damage.

The coroner's men carry red plastic toolboxes. Through binoculars I see what might be hair or intestines or something unraveling. The men's bright orange jackets have *coroner* written in silver neon tape across the back. I put the binoculars down.

My son knows better than to look.

I find a shoe in the park that skirts the highway and want to know if it belongs to the person who walked into traffic that night. I check online for some kind of report but don't find anything.

From my bedroom window I watch the icebreakers on the Hudson. At night their lights illuminate the ripples in the water. The tallest trees bend into the wind and I am grateful I no longer live in the house of my childhood.

Pigeons normally do not come up this high and I have never seen one perched on the narrow ledge outside my window. Its snow-laden feathers press against its body and glisten as if covered in oil. As it shivers its beak taps the window. I put my head against the glass. We are eye to eye.

The boy's mother cradles him in her lap and whispers to him in Quechua. A bag of dextrose and antibiotics hangs from a pole. She watches his chest rise and fall. Her lips are moving. I think she is counting each breath as if she knows how many are left.

His tie-on cotton top with tiny yellow and blue triangles turns red. The blood from his chest tube saturates the cloth. Her cry for help reaches the waiting room and echoes through the corridor. The surgeon, summoned from the operating room, whisks the boy from her. She needs me to stay, to keep speaking, as if my presence will influence the outcome.

The boy survives. But the surgery doesn't accomplish what was intended. He will leave the way he came, only weaker and traumatized. His mother is distraught knowing that once we are gone, there will be no one else.

On our last day the doctors and nurses, the packed equipment and remaining supplies are piled into the bus, the one the Ministry of Health made available to us with the headlights drawn onto a wooden board affixed to the front, most likely to keep the engine from toppling out. A woman with a child strapped across her back bangs on the bus door. I know I am late, she says, but please.

My son insists we open the door. Exhausted as we are, he asks us to give her some piece of advice.

The bus driver stops at a cinderblock structure with a corrugated roof. It is good luck when leaving to say a prayer at this shrine. Christ on the crucifix hangs from the far wall, having washed ashore in 2003, a remnant from a shipwreck nearly two hundred years ago. Yet the blood, especially on the right side of his face, is a vibrant red as if painted yesterday.

The young girl who came each night to the barn where I lived with the blonde man has her own family now. Her oldest son was hit by a truck while riding his bicycle on the Pan American Highway and is paralyzed from the neck down.

She built a shrine at the place of the accident. A wooden box on top of a pole painted blue that looks something like a birdhouse, decorated with plastic flowers. She lights candles at the base each week and prays for him to walk again. The boy is my son's age to the day. Her other children feed, carry and clean him.

My son hooks the television into the cable connection and winds the wires behind the molding. His laptop is bolted to the table. I have made the bed. The dormitory walls are unpainted cinderblock.

He walks us in the direction of the car. None of us remember exactly where we parked. It is a humid, Washington D.C., end-of-August day.

I hug my son. I do not linger but pull away. I open the door and drop into the passenger seat.

My husband and son continue talking outside on the pavement. It is terribly hot inside the car and I gesture to my husband. He knows I do not have the keys and cannot open the window. I tap the glass and motion again.

I look in the rear-view mirror hoping I will see my son walking away, just the back of his shirt, even the heel of his sneaker, but before I can focus I am taken by a raspy, clawing sound. My husband, now seated behind the wheel, is crying. It is the sort of crying he must have done as a child that so unnerved his mother, where his whole body quaked.

Turn on the car so the air conditioning can get going.

It's a long drive.
The traffic in D.C. is terrible.
Especially on Sunday evening.

Each time the leaving is different. The distance further.

Dig deep and there is water. Men wrapped in rags tend hectares of green tendrils in perfectly ordered rows. Then the green abruptly ends and there is sand.

The winter in Lima, my son says, is unusual on account of *el Niño*. When I was there it ravaged the coast, I tell him. Whole villages washed away and malaria spread to areas that had never before been affected. A friend shivering and sweating, pale as a sheet, was hardly recognizable.

After I left for Lima I never returned to my parent's house, not even for one night, not when they were sick and needed my help.

The farmer gives me a roll of pink plastic to mark the trees I want to buy. Between the farmer's shed and his shuttered house I hear what sounds like an animal in pain. Inside an old pickup is a boy, his body twisted and gnarled, his face distorted. I put my hands over my ears to block out his cries, but even if the windows had been rolled up, the whole valley would have heard.

I never return for the tagged trees, the red maple, the peach, and the apple that would have bloomed so beautifully in my backyard.

In the middle of the night I wrap the dying dog in a towel and drag her to the car. Two men from the hospital come outside and lift her onto a dog gurney.

The veterinarian tells us it is time. My son begs him to make sure there is nothing else that can be done. The potato chips and ground beef I brought from home have no effect. Blood from the meat oozes out of the tin foil leaving a circular stain on the floor. Already, she is so still.

Hours after the injection my son is still petting her, his head buried in the folds of her neck. At three a.m. I touch his back. It's time to go, I say, before reaching over to lift him off of her. Her cold hard body makes me pull back.

I pick up a wooden box shaped like a house, nailed shut, with the dog's name etched on a metal plate. I don't know what to do with it. First I put it on the mantelpiece, then in a desk drawer, before moving it to the basement. When my son notices it is missing I ask him to please take it.

The mud houses come into view as the plane begins its descent into Lima. My son made tiny houses of mud from a brick-making kit, mixing the sand and gravel into mortar. When the consistency was right he poured it into miniature plastic molds, then stacked and glued the bricks in place. He constructed houses, a school, towers, corrals and sidewalks. If he didn't like what he made he chiseled the bricks free, soaked them in water and started again.

After everything was in its place, glued to a board, he drew a map marking the location of the roads and buildings.

It isn't understood how the ancient *Colla* moved the massive boulders or how they aligned and stacked them to construct the many-storied cylindrical funeral towers that border Lake Titicaca.

We peer through the cracks in the stone and see the vertical holes dug into the earth where the bodies, wrapped in woven shrouds, were once fitted in the upright position facing east.

Mummified bodies, mostly of small children excavated at the site, were moved to temperature-controlled vaults in the capital. It is unclear if the children were sacrificed or if they died of natural causes.

The placement of the stones is the same for every tower, even those miles away and on opposite shores of Lake Titicaca.

I want to tell a group of Brazilians to take their revelry elsewhere, to remind them we are in an ancient graveyard. They do not bother my son who is more concerned about the fate of an injured llama we passed on the road tied to a spindly pine tree, its hind leg wrapped in an Indian woman's woven belt. Even from the car window we could see the bone was not set properly. My son keeps asking what is the value of a pack animal with a broken leg?

When he was sick he worried the animals were not safe. Where and which ones I didn't know, but each week he watched as I wrote a check to a charity he determined sufficiently dedicated to helping hurt and abandoned animals. He kept a spreadsheet in his top desk drawer to be sure the money was equitably distributed.

Early accounts of expeditions in the vicinity of Titicaca detail headaches suffered by the explorers, reporting a terrifying sleeplessness. Even though their bodies were exhausted their minds could not rest. Stones carved with the names of those who died were wedged horizontally into the earth, the coordinates noted.

Unable to climb the hill of the most impressive tower I tell my son he needs to go alone. The sun is beating down but it is the altitude, and I do not mean just to the towers. It is that I must leave.

He would rush out the front door into the busy street, half-naked to avoid a bath. But then it became much more. It wasn't just the bath; rain, even melting snow, any feeling of wet.

Nausea follows my loss of appetite. The pain pulses directly behind my eyes. Exhaustion and lack of oxygen produce a hyper-wakefulness. My thinking and movements have slowed. Each motion is broken down into individual steps and it is increasingly difficult to complete even a simple task.

My son helps me pack my bag and tie my shoelaces. I leave medicine in the bathroom and my sweater in the restaurant. In slow, tortured motion, I tumble through space.

The first months of nursery school I am the only parent on the child-sized chair in the corner of the room. All the other children adjusted to being left. If I got up, even to approach the door, my son's body became rigid and his eyes bore deep into mine, pleading with me to sit back down.

I insist he does not accompany me to the airport. As the cab driver and I get closer the streets are clogged with striking miners, tanks and other military vehicles. It does not occur to me that the government might shut down the airport.

Maybe the llama had been abandoned and will die of starvation, and even if someone were to return, it would likely be to slaughter it.

I stand outside on the concrete slab under a makeshift tin roof. An employee in a yellow jump suit with the name of the airline stenciled across the back pushes a sign. Scribbled in chalk is the flight number and final destination. As we are boarding, I imagine him pushing the sign back into the storage closet, removing his work clothes and locking the door.

As soon as the cabin fills with oxygen I fall into a deep sleep, the first since arriving at Titicaca.

The summer before kindergarten my son collected and catalogued hundreds of rocks, displaying each one on my mother-in-law's card tables, which he dragged from the basement to the backyard, the laminated tops collapsed flush against the hollow, folded legs. When each leg was locked in place, he shimmied it into the dirt.

He knew where he found each rock and marked the spot on a hand-drawn map. In the same composition book he kept a record of each one's weight, its surface area, and thickness.

Because my handwriting was better than his he asked me to write on a piece of plywood with a thick black marker: Museum of Stones with an arrow pointing toward the tables. We mounted the sign on a stake and planted it alongside the road so cars passing by could see it.

Each morning he assembled the stones in the same configuration, predominantly linear but with distinct piles arranged in carefully composed circles.

We dismantled the tables at sunset. He carried each rock to an open tarp positioned under the porch. I followed with the larger rocks. If it looked as if it might rain my mother-in-law would help, walking behind me, a rock in each hand.

By the end of August we had flattened a path of grass from the tables to the porch with our processioning.

Grandmother asked if he had a favorite. Pointing to the front row, she said, this series of configurations is my favorite part, the way each stone is perfectly smooth and how even in its blackness it still reflects light.

When the stones were set and ordered properly for the night my son brought the plastic corners of the tarp into the center and placed a protective brick on top. He turned back to be certain we hadn't forgotten any.

He was up from bed calling to me as he was pulling on his pants. One of the rocks, his voice quivered, one of Grandma's favorites, I forgot to bring inside and I dreamed when I went to pick it up, it split in half, imperfectly, making it impossible for me to fit it back together. I tell him it is too dark to go outside, that we will check first thing in the morning.

At sea level I eat and drink freely. The evening news is flooded with footage of the protests in and around Titicaca. Crowds of people covered in blood, their clothing torn, try to make their way out of the chaos. The worst violence is near the airport where my son needs to be.

He doesn't arrive in Lima as planned. I call his cellphone but either there is no service or his phone has gone dead.

I do not feel the impact but the cab driver must have hit the beggar walking towards us as we approached a stop sign. The man limps to the side of the road dropping the roses from the highlands he was trying to sell. Red petals that could be mistaken for blood fall across the pavement. I tell the driver to stop, that we need to make sure the man doesn't need our help.

In the dream my son is on an inflatable, not a sturdy seaworthy one, something similar to the pink, plastic floats we blew up and floated in the bath. I am able to see him but he cannot see me. I knock on the thick pane of glass separating us, desperate to get his attention. His float pitches on a dark sea. I turn away for a moment and when I look back, he and the inflatable are gone.

In the middle of the night my cell phone rings. I hesitate as I walk toward it. If I do not answer, whatever it is that has happened will not become present.

No one is on the line.

I am unable to get back to sleep.

Two days late, now bathed and wrapped in a robe from the hotel, my son orders room service, a combination of lunch and breakfast and dessert. He tells me the only meat he was offered the five days he was in Bolivia was llama. On the third day, weak and lightheaded, thinking he needed protein, he took a bite, but spit it half-chewed into his napkin.

He packed by candlelight then dipped each finger into the wax, carefully removing the hardened, molded tips. Ordered in a line, he left them on the hotel nightstand, far better than dental records.

The hotel arranged for a driver to take him in the middle of the night to the other side of the lake in an inflatable equipped with an outboard motor. During the day the lake was patrolled by the military and crossing into Peru was prohibited. It was so dark he could not see even the outline of his body. As the water breached the sides, his toes, then legs, numbed. There were no life preservers, only a set of emergency paddles rattling against each other. His biggest fear was they might abrade the inflated plastic hull.

A seagull shat on his head but he didn't dare wipe it, as this would have required letting go of the cord that ran along the side of the boat.

Straining for the shoreline to come into view, he hallucinated its appearance many times.

In the inky blackness there was no demarcation of water from sky. He felt he was watching himself spinning through a vortex propelled by wind and a battering current in a world comprised of water, a piece of plastic, a bit of metal, and a boy.

The trip took over three hours and in that time the moon never appeared from behind a thick covering of clouds.

The Zodiac driver pointed to a car waiting on the shore that would take him on the final stretch of his journey. He was so numb and the land so covered in fog he wasn't sure any of it was real.

He saw ghosts rising from the funeral towers, each blanketed in a thick, gray mist. They appeared as women, their hair dripping with lake water that formed puddles around their ivory colored feet. Hands clasped, they made a long line that wound up the face of the mountain. If someone were on the top looking down it would have looked as if tiny birds were falling.

Halfway through his meal he gets up and goes to the window. A hairless dog howls in the courtyard. He asks how long the dog has been tied up, then calls the front desk and demands that something be done, repeating that the dog has no shade or food or water. The receptionist tells him what she has been telling me all week, the hotel doesn't have access to the lot, that there is nothing she can do.

Inside the box are drawings from his years of pre-school, his first pair of shoes, the black and white zebra and the *New York Times* from the day he was born.

In a separate plastic container are the primary colors of thousands of Legos, the partially deconstructed shapes he fashioned into houses and skyscrapers. I dig amongst the pieces to reach a scrap of paper, hoping he left some sort of clue. But it is only a cancelled check I wrote to a local dog shelter.

Kindergarten was crayons and construction paper, tubs of salty glue we nibbled from when the teacher wasn't looking. I didn't feel sick but vomited in the middle of the drawing and used the palm of my hand to blend it in as if it were part of the design.

No one heard me choke and no one asked why I could not stop rubbing the paper.

My mother-in-law has a tin stuffed with old birthday cards addressed to my husband and folded pages of colored construction paper with the stick-like figures he drew. In separate time zones we learned green, blue and yellow from a box of eight crayons. Marley is written in red across every sky, the name of his make-believe friend.

I wrote love letters to myself and signed them David. There was a boy with that name in school. He was shorter than all the other boys. I practiced writing as I imagined a boy might write, messy and without proper punctuation.

From the mailbox on the corner of Main Street I mailed myself the letters I wrote, passing the blue metal receptacle on my way home from school. Mother never noticed that some of her stamps were missing. Sometimes I would stop to watch and imagined David holding down the shelf and slipping the white envelope inside.

No one asked what I was holding, even though I carried the letters with me in full view, folding and unfolding them before carefully sliding the pencil-written page into the soiled, well-worn envelope.

A blue car pulled over – I had just finished mailing a David letter – and a man motioned for me to approach the open passenger-side window. The man was rubbing his hand between his legs. Before I realized what he was doing I had already started running.

I never mailed another David letter.

I spent the afternoon in a police car trying to find the man in the blue car. The siren wasn't on and we didn't speed as the officer took me through the suburban streets of symmetrical hedges and whimsical mailboxes.

The policeman asked questions I couldn't answer and after a while he took me home without us finding what I remembered to be a large blue car with silver headlights.

That night Mother let me keep the light on. In the morning I was still afraid but she no longer had time for me and told me to get dressed for school.

We had been told to be kind to a girl in my Sunday school class who had a terrible stutter. She walked crooked, as if she was pulling away, or leaning into the wind, even hoping it would carry her off. She had been gang-raped by a horde of boys when she got off the bus in fifth grade. We weren't sure what this meant and there was endless speculation. When the boys were done they left her in a ditch.

I come across a rudimentary beehive shape made of clay, glazed in blue and orange as we are cleaning out my mother-in-law's room in the old age home. I hold it with both hands, turn it around, and run my fingers along the coils. Mother-in-law used it to store safety pins and scraps of paper. Not until I turn it over and see my son's initials carved by an adult do I realize why it caught my attention. I wrap it in a tattered washcloth and put it in my pocketbook.

My in-laws sold their house years earlier and it has since changed hands a number of times. The tarp covering the rocks was likely one of the first things to be thrown out. The smooth and creviced stones, the black ones and the ones with mica running through would now be part of the ground cover or partially buried.

I have a pink float I pull from the pool each night, washing it with the hose before I lean it against the patio wall. In the morning I set it adrift and watch as it moves across the water, silently propelled by the wind.

The Inca believed the souls of the dead rose to the mountains, that lightning was evidence of their power.

I follow a boy from a nearby apartment building to the dog park. His features are similar to those of the boy whose face is papered across the city. He sits on the bench and watches. He is not gaunt and starved, which is how I imagine the missing boy, gone now for over two weeks.

He extends his arms outward for the dogs. Many come to him, their tails wagging. When he has their attention he throws the tennis ball, and they go running.

My mother ordered my son to sit on his great-grandmother's lap. He accidently touched her hair and his body arched as he pulled away. It was weightless, he told me, hollow like straw. For many years he believed the hair emptying out was the last thing to happen before someone died.

After a child's arm washes ashore in Queens a search is underway for the rest of the missing boy.

A woman in a red blazer circles back, mumbling a meeting is about to begin, that it cannot be missed. She returns again and again, having no memory of just delivering the same message. On our next visit she is no longer circling. Mother-in-law heard they sent her to a different old-age home, one for those who can't remember.

After my mother-in-law's funeral my husband and I drive to his childhood home. I ring the doorbell but no one is there. Under the porch I find what I believe to be a pile of stones from the Museum of Stones. I fill my pocket with these stones.

When her gravestone was unveiled one year later I placed one of the stones from the Museum of Stones – the one that looked most like the one I remembered she preferred – across the Hebrew lettering of her name, as is the tradition.

The boy in the bed next to my son died the day before Thanksgiving. I watched as his father ran his fingers over the large gold *Chai* he wore around his neck. *Chai,* and its promise of life had failed him.

A week earlier I stood behind the father in the admitting line when I remembered the woman's last name, the one who gave my husband the desk lamp, his occasional golf partner, Nastsis. Like mosquitoes.

I shook my arm to rid myself of the fly or the gnat, but nothing was there.

The blonde man killed a wild turkey on a Thursday in November, thinking it was Thanksgiving back home. Hikers from the States on their way to the highest mountain stopped at our hut to inquire about the weather. Because snow was expected they decided to wait. We invited them to celebrate with us.

I boiled yams and cooked the turkey in an outdoor pit lined with eucalyptus and pine. As we sat down to eat the snow was beginning to fall.

Does the dead son's father have other sons? It would matter I think, but I can't say how. I have only seen his wife.

I take a seat in the front pew of the hospital chapel. Others weep as they pray. I do not know how to pray but I can weep. My sorrow spreads across the room, fills the empty spaces, writes a spider's web of condensation on the glass. The moisture slides down, moving the way tears fall, starting and stopping in a trickle and then flowing in a quickly moving stream.

My brother buys his wife a Mercedes wagon. Their matching Wedgewood china, selected in advance, is stacked in padded pouches and stored on the top shelf of the pantry. His daughter is a musical prodigy. The younger one, a son, is best known for having jumped roof-to-roof, tossing bricks into the street.

His wife glances at the cast that runs the length of her right arm. She mumbles, as no one would dare ask, it was a bike accident. The roof jumper makes it to appetizers, then, without provocation becomes enraged. His mother gets up, maintaining her composure as she walks to the bathroom.

My brother tries to reason with him, which is what he always does. At dessert his wife rejoins us, ordering the apple pie. I would have run farther than the bathroom and I would not have returned.

I use the blade of the butter knife to move the crumbs left, then right. What I remember of my brother's wife's childhood home, where we went each Thanksgiving, are the empty rooms with the lights turned off and the eerie silence from no one talking, the humming of the fluorescent tubes.

When my son was very sick we were blamed for having done something wrong or for not having done enough. My husband's father tried to console us by saying there are so many things we cannot control.

My son remembers the time of boarded windows, chains and padlocks. The absences, how I didn't come home or call, leaving him with Fuckitfret, who was useless, possibly dangerous as her driving was worse than mine. The way I was at home but was not present. The vomit in my hair, the unexplained bruises.

My husband's youngest sister's wedding dress has a train seven times her height, making it difficult for her and the dress to fit in the back of her father's Chevy Vega. En route to the ceremony, perched on the edge of the seat, the train and veil encircle her. The expression on her face is of childlike wonder.

Our breath clouds the front windshield. The defroster isn't working and I am afraid my husband is having trouble seeing the road. Rain begins to fall in slanted lines. I glance back to see if she is nervous. She is floating above the seat, her dress a parachute that has deployed.

I buy our nanny her wedding dress, a knockoff from a designer style made in China. At fittings with her and her bridesmaids I worry that if someone were to light a match all of us would go up in flames, the smell of acetate asphyxiating.

My mother-in-law points out various residents and refers to them by their previous vocations, the judge, a cardiologist, the one who sang soprano.

The last living male in the home has lung disease and when we visit even if it is raining or snowing we find him in the parking lot in his wheelchair, staring at the traffic smoking. He parks his tank of oxygen, strapped to a stand with two wheels in the breezeway of the building. I wonder what he thinks about as he sits in the cold Canadian winter, hastening his death.

Boys especially taunt my son. They are Power Ranger and Star Wars obsessed, while he is confirming the symmetry of a sunflower's seeded center, making notes in his spiral composition book.

For years he strapped around his waist a satchel filled with essential items. After he left home, I find the satchel in the bottom of his desk drawer. At first I throw it into the trash but, later that evening, I pull it out and go through it. Inside is a book on the Yeti, his Swiss army knife and a dehydrated ice cream sandwich from the Museum of Natural History.

Other parents were sending their children to camp. My husband objected concerned it would be too regimented. Nonetheless, I signed him up. Every morning was a struggle. Midway into the summer after pushing him out of the car I decided to stay and gauge how bad.

The other kids joked with one another while my son was off to the side, unengaged, his expression so frozen I thought maybe he wasn't mine.

Without stopping to collect his things, I should have gone inside and taken him by the hand and led him to the car so he could have felt the freedom that comes from leaving. Instead, I turned and walked away, and in the car cried self-serving tears.

The bus driver had no choice but to pull over to the side of the road to get the campers under control, pushing them one by one into their seats. The stress and chaos might be why my son wet his pants, but the doctor insisted on a sonogram to make sure his kidneys were functioning properly. I stood in the half-lit room, wondering if it was better if something was physically wrong with him.

A school bus stops at the light. A lone child in the last row looks out the window. It is the first week back after Christmas break when there is little to look forward to, the hours of daylight are short, and the streets are strewn with desiccated Christmas trees, leftover pieces of tinsel and discarded boughs.

The child's face brightens when she points to my dog. I turn the dog's head towards her closed window, thinking if he sees her, he will respond, but he does not look up. Her smile fades as she presses her face and hands against the glass.

Heaving breath-stealing sobs, a boy stops in the middle of the street. His mother pulls at him as the light changes. It was an awful day, he repeats, refusing to pick up his feet. The rubber of his sneakers squeals as he drags them across the asphalt.

Great-grandmother changed my grandfather's first name to elude the angel of death. But the infection in the bones of his legs continued to spread. She carried him from village to village, consoling him with stories of sundrenched plains and hand-painted tiles, counting in her seven different languages.

I asked what languages. Grandfather told me what mattered was the rhythm, not the words, that they were the lullabies and songs of the gypsies.

The night he died he wanted no morphine. In a clear, strong voice, he called out his mother's name in Yiddish: Yetta.

Suburban houses of white clapboard line the route, some with porches attached to the back, others with plastic blow-up pools. A green plastic hose, window boxes of ivy and pots of geraniums, leaves caught in the bric-a-brac hammered around the underbelly.

When the gym teacher thought my son was in some other world he was keeping track of numbers, counting and cataloging vast systems in his head. Sports did not interest him but the fantastic swirl of calculations did.

A *quipu* is made of a thick cotton cord from which thinner cords are suspended. Each contains clusters of knots arranged in a decimal system. The Inca used them for keeping records, births and deaths, years of rain and drought.

My husband told himself stories when he was a child while he rocked up and down in bed, knees drawn to his chest. Stories of nothing, he said. When I persisted he told me he went over in his mind a famous hat trick, three goals in one hockey game. The excitement in the stands was so great the fans stood in unison and threw their hats into the rink. The number of the player's shirt, the one who performed the hat trick, became my husband's lucky number.

Tiny chairs squat to the ground with rectangular child-sized seats are brought to my mother-in-law's apartment and placed in a line. When the seven days of mourning are over the men return to collect the chairs. They will be stored in the synagogue basement for the next family of mourners.

The chair sitters are given a safety pin and a piece of torn black crepe. My husband and his sisters wear the same shirt and crepe for seven days. They are not supposed to go outside or cook or bathe. They are to mourn.

Children from the Andes, the desert, and as far east as the jungle sit on their parents' laps, nearly blind from the combination of altitude, dust and sun. They are so many they spill into the hallway, yet they are not loud or impatient. So unlike children in a waiting room back home.

No child takes more than his or her share of juice and cookies. And when the snacks are finished, a thin boy with crossed-eyes walks from family to family with a plastic bag collecting the wrappers. His left shoe is not the same as the one on his right foot.

My son unknowingly wore his shoes on the wrong feet and I would have to tell him to switch them. But it didn't impair his mobility. He established a distance from his corporeal self as he moved through space.

We are at my husband's sister's house when my father-in-law soils himself. My mother-in-law calls for my husband, who is paralyzed with fear, whereas my husband's middle sister, the one who stashes cookies and leftover food in a canvas bag, eating when everyone is asleep, washes my father-in-law and dresses him in clean clothes. Midweek she gets up from her *shiva* chair and announces she is done.

She held my husband's head the first time he drank too much scotch and smoked too many cigars in the now-dead father's den. I see him and his friends seated on the aquamarine plastic couch, the upholstered orange chairs, their middle-school acne, long hair and ponytails, smelling of alcohol and smoke.

From the window I watch the cruise ships dock. During my father-in-law's last year my mother-in-law sat at this same spot while they held hands, inventing new lives for the visitors disembarking in their colored shorts and floppy hats, money belts strapped to their waists.

She made him take walks around the wharf. People came up to them and when they engaged my father-in-law in conversation they realized his mind was gone.

Something in his eyes told her he understood as she explained his sister had died, yet as the day progressed he said, I feel so sad today, more so than ever, but have no idea why.

A woman in northern Canada saw my father-in-law's obituary. Thirty years ago she was living in the hospital room of her sick son when my mother-in-law brought her home, driving her each day to the hospital and back. And as if it were yesterday the woman is calling to express her condolences and to once again thank my mother-in-law for her kindness.

The last day of *shiva* my husband's youngest sister has to get out of the house. She takes my hand and tells me we are going to King's Street. At the bottom of King's Street is the only jewelry store in the town. I am wearing the necklace my husband gave me when my son was born. I follow her inside. She says, my father took me here and had the owner bring out whatever I wanted to try on. She points to my neck and asks the salesperson to please clean the diamond.

A certain shaped skipping stone makes me cry.

My son was with him when he died.
My husband was in the hallway talking to a high school friend.
His sisters and mother were having coffee.

My son stayed behind to wipe the spittle that dribbled from the old man's mouth, using squares of sterilized gauze.

There was no death rattle or any other sound, just a pallor that moved down his face, passing over his checks, engulfing his hands. It wasn't until the monitor began its incessant beeping that he knew for sure.

Each night after sitting all day with them on their tiny chairs I woke covered in welts. By morning there would be no bites or raised areas, only the blood caked under my nails from scratching.

When the days of mourning are over we miss our connecting flight home. The only motel is on the turnpike across from the airport. It is midday and we are in a town so desolate we cannot buy even a book. Staring at the linoleum ceiling tiles we debate renting a car and driving for eighteen hours just to be moving.

My son finds a movie theatre in a nearby mall. The best choice is about a brown stuffed bear that comes to life. Because he saw his grandfather die I am afraid the story might send him back to childhood.

His anaerobic digester is up and running in a number of villages in South America, powering cook stoves and electric bulbs. Alongside the digester he rigged a panel for capturing energy produced by the movement of the children on seesaws.

At first they didn't know what a seesaw was and needed to be shown. He saw how delighted they were and bought cans of paint and paintbrushes so they could decorate them. The older children drew the outlines of large birds across the planks and helped the younger ones keep the paint within the lines.

He shows me a photograph of a boy with his handmade pull toy, a truck cobbled together from an empty can and bottle caps. The boy watched the assembly of the digester and then the positioning and wiring of the seesaw panels. The next day he replicated it using twigs and straw. I wonder what that child is doing now.

Grandfather's only amusement as a child was a cloth book in Russian. It told the story of a boat.

My son hid a cell phone under a ceiling tile and during biology class called the phone from his seat. The teacher who ridiculed the students, especially the ones that struggled, rushed around looking for the origin of the sound. If she were close my son ended the call. Once she regained her composure and returned to her notes, he dialed again.

The organization sends shirts for the doctors and nurses with dates of the medical team's tour of duty written across the back. The shirts go missing from a locked supply cabinet.

As my son discharges the children he hands the parents and guardians follow-up instructions, bottles of medicine and a shirt wrapped in brown paper, tied with string. He explains they shouldn't open the package until they are on the bus heading home.

It isn't until the trip administrator suggests it was likely a Peruvian who took the shirts that a look of regret passes over my son's face.

Many children were processed through Theresienstadt. Their drawings are similar to those hanging in the United Nations' lobby drawn by children in Sudan. Peacocks and butterflies, a sun and then something terrible, a gun, or a body on the ground, blood-covered.

When we leave our hotel in Prague it is a hot September day with full sun. By afternoon the sky is dull and the streets of Theresienstadt are gray, the houses too. The landscape looks as if it has been exposed to Chernobyl-grade radiation.

An old woman sells eggs out of the back of a truck. Our tour guide points to her and says the only people who would live here alongside the ghosts are the gypsies.

Nervously I kick the soil. I imagine deep in the ground amongst the ash from the crematorium are shards of broken pottery and scraps of leather from tattered soles.

My son and I sit on the dirt floor and cut pieces of cake with the Swiss-army knife we brought from home. We place each slice on a piece of ruled school paper and eat with our fingers. The boy's sister puts small bites into her paralyzed brother's mouth, while his mother, the girl I once read to many years ago, holds his neck straight so he will not choke.

I notice my son's left sneaker is worn in the same place as mine.

We drive to what was a lake when I lived here and is now a muddy expanse littered in goose shit. We pass abandoned mud huts with thatched roofs, one after the other, until I lose count.

An old man sits on the ground sorting kernels of corn. I ask where everyone has gone. When the water dried up, the adults left for Lima, for Barcelona, any place they could go where they heard there might be jobs, leaving their children, promising they would send for them when they were able.

When no one returned, when there were no remittances, some children migrated to the city to become beggars or worse, while others were, initially, taken in by evangelicals.

There is one hut that is intact where a worn shirt dries on a tree branch. I call inside. Two boys come out into the light looking starved and nearly mad, their eyes sunken into their foreheads. They can't say how long their parents have been gone but they are waiting.

After the Madrid bombings, the charred body of an immigrant from Peru is found in a parked car.

The only item my son will bring home is a sponge. The sponges in Lima are well constructed, thicker than paper towel with excellent absorbency, but thinner than the average kitchen sponge.

Seated at his desk looking out at the city he hears a noise so loud he is sure whatever it is has broken the window. At first he fears it is a bullet. When he sees the splattered blood with a feather dangling, he realizes the bird must have been flying at lightning speed.

A bullet-like radius of concentric circles emanates from the place of impact. The glass, however, remains intact. He needs me to convince him it was an accident, that the bird did not commit suicide.

After the hurricane my husband and I emerge from the house wearing our bike helmets, afraid of falling debris. There are piles of stones at the bottom of the drive, swept down by the torrential rain.

A man undresses in the corner of the subway on the lower level before the stairs, partially hidden from view. I look away, not wanting to see him in his underwear, or worse, but a flash of red makes me turn back. He is dressing in an Elmo costume.

A perfect loaf of bread with an **F** engraved on top must have fallen from someone's grocery bag and been kicked the length of the subway car. I do not want to be on the train when a homeless person reaches under the seat and rests it in the crook of his arm.

Standing across from me is a Chinese man carrying a huge see-through garbage bag. I could never estimate the amount of candy corn or jellybeans in a jar, but I would have liked to say approximately how many fortunes he held.

Two pairs of saddle-shoed feet poke out of a carriage. Size two, I would guess. I had no idea you could still buy such shoes. Buster Brown was the name of the company when my mother bought them for my sister and me. In the insole there was a picture of a boy and his dog.

I want to ask the woman in charge of the stroller if it would be possible to take off just one of the children's shoes so I could look inside.

How many times have I said my son's name?

I walk beside him, occasionally falling a few steps behind. The air is humid and heavy.

They were always Velcro and as a result, my son still has no idea how to tie a shoelace.

He had eaten too much candy at the Halloween party. I pulled the car to the side of the road. He dropped to his knees and was sick. When it was over, he got back into the car and sat peacefully, like a soapstone Buddha.

I find the book of milestones I kept until I realized he wasn't meeting them.

He should hold onto my books even though I understand he will have concerns of space and mold, and why would he or whomever he might be living with want to be burdened by my things?

How cumbersome his possessions became, everything he stashed and stored, that years later I tossed into so many dumpsters.

No. I cannot ask him. I will throw all of it out.

A child's shoe washes ashore in a distant country.

A man so exhausted he looks ancient, carries his son on his shoulders. They continue in what they hope is a forward direction. Likely they will arrive at locked gates and barbed wire coiled above concrete walls.

A woman and her newborn son drown en route.

The tunnel comes to a dead stop. Steps are retraced. A different direction discussed. They do not know how to choose. To travel nameless from a nameless place, to call out your name and where you are from when you fear you will not survive. Your last hope is someone who does survive will hear and remember your name so at the very least, those left behind will know to stop waiting.

Documents my son must make sense of in order to complete his dissertation are dumped in a warehouse on the outskirts of Lima.

Even in Peru, bureaucrats do not have it in them to destroy the papers they are charged with producing.

There are no shelves, not even a surface where he might spread the documents side by side and begin to implement a procedure for organizing them. No file folders or cabinets, not even rubber bands. Still, he is confident he will uncover the information he has been trying to find for years.

In the mayor's office in Ica, Peru the walls are lime green. There is an upholstered matching green velvet couch. On it sit different sizes of stuffed bears. All of them are Winnie the Pooh. My son and I confirm we both saw this.

Mold is everywhere and multiplies because of the humid winter. This year is far more humid than any year on record. He buys a HAZMAT suit, a mask and gloves, and begins in what seems a logical place, the far-left corner of the rectangular building.

Days run into months. He develops a rash that encrusts his skin, oozing yellow muck. His lungs become infected. His sinuses need to be drained. He has to throw his clothing away.

Peering out from my protective eyewear I snap on the rubber gloves, pin on the hairnet and step into an extra small protective suit.

Tomorrow we will bring a ladder, more bottles of water, wipes, and toilet paper so we can relieve ourselves out back amongst the beggars and the homeless.

He is writing in his notebook and doesn't look up. There has to be a way to reconfigure, some other protection, a better mask to wear.

My eyes are smarting, my nose running. The dust scrapes my throat.

I say his name but he is deep within the piles. Perhaps he has solved a piece of the riddle. It is possible the whole thing is coming into focus.

I walk into the alleyway. Take off the HAZMAT suit, the gloves and drop them on the ground. I know when the flights leave Lima for New York. I continue in the direction of the hotel although it is miles from where I am.

I pass the mangy dogs, the children with distended bellies, the flies hovering above the rut in the road filled with filthy water.

I look into the murky puddle, a skim of oil reflecting on its surface. All the pieces of my face are where they are supposed to be, no distortions or duplications, not even when I drop a pebble and watch the water ripple outward.

ABOUT THE AUTHOR

LYNN LURIE is the author of three novels, *Corner of the Dead* (2008), winner of the Juniper Prize, *Quick Kills* (2014), which Brian Evenson described as "filled with quiet menace" and *Museum of Stones* (2018).

Books from Etruscan Press

Etruscan Press Is Proud of Support Received From

Wilkes University

Youngstown State University

The Raymond John Wean Foundation

The Ohio Arts Council

The Stephen & Jeryl Oristaglio Foundation

The Nathalie & James Andrews Foundation

The National Endowment for the Arts

The Ruth H. Beecher Foundation

The Bates-Manzano Fund

The New Mexico Community Foundation

Founded in 2001 with a generous grant from the Oristaglio Foundation, Etruscan Press is a nonprofit cooperative of poets and writers working to produce and promote books that nurture the dialogue among genres, achieve a distinctive voice, and reshape the literary and cultural histories of which we are a part.

etruscan press
www.etruscanpress.org

Etruscan Press books may be ordered from

Consortium Book Sales and Distribution
800.283.3572
www.cbsd.com

Etruscan Press is a 501(c)(3) nonprofit organization.
Contributions to Etruscan Press are tax deductible
as allowed under applicable law.
For more information, a prospectus,
or to order one of our titles,
contact us at books@etruscanpress.org.